PRAISE FOR JO

"Joan's dry wit is downright hilarious, sometimes unintentionally, sometimes as a coping mechanism. . . . Wang doesn't mute Joan's rage, but leaves it always bubbling under the surface. . . . It's there in her sly comebacks to . . . low-key racism and attempts to dehumanize her. . . . Through funny, weird and touching moments, Wang depicts . . . grief as messy, non-linear and palpable. . . . In taut prose, Wang masterfully balances the many terrors of this pandemic alongside Joan's intimate, interior struggles [and] raises provocative questions about motherhood, daughterhood, belonging and the many definitions of 'home.' What do we owe our parents? Our children? And are any of us OK?"

—*The New York Times Book Review*

"By exploring the spectrum of commitment—from doubts about one's career and cultural identity, as depicted in Wang's debut novel *Chemistry,* to a deep passion for one's calling that seems tantamount to faith in *Joan Is Okay*—Weike Wang has shown us myriad ways to build a sense of home, myriad ways to feel okay in our skin."

—NPR

"Joan is an irresistibly quirky—and strong—character helming a wry, wise and simply spectacular book."

—*People* (Book of the Week)

"Engaging and funny . . . In Joan, Wang has created a compelling character, utterly distinct, and the novel is carried by her dispassionate, clear-eyed, and often drily amusing narration. [The book's] powerful insights will resonate with many."

—Claire Messud, *Harper's*

"Rarely has cross-cultural bewilderment been rendered more hilariously, or with such understated poignancy. . . . It's remarkable how much Wang packs into her beguilingly quick and readable 224 pages: a story of immigrant aspiration, a medically informed reflection on the pandemic, a portrait of a woman trying to figure out the culture into which she was born by watching *Seinfeld,* and an examination of why someone might not want to be different (or, for that matter, indifferent)."
—Pico Iyer, *Air Mail*

"Wang's dry wit . . . is irresistible."
—*Chicago Tribune* (Best Books of 2022)

"Spare yet humorous, this is a moving portrait of a woman navigating misogyny and xenophobia as she attempts to find her place in the world."
—*Harper's Bazaar*

"A smart, powerful, and very contemporary read that touches on the sorts of struggles that are shaping the very world we live in today."
—*Town & Country*

"I was lucky enough to get my hands on a review copy of this novel. . . . The quirky protagonist reminded me of some people in my family, who don't always "get" social norms but are fully themselves, and you love them all the more for it. . . . Wang's debut *Chemistry* won eight gazillion awards, and I won't be surprised if this [novel] does, too."
—Joanna Goddard, *Cup of Jo*

"Wang's sense of humor makes this both a page-turner and a poignant reflection on the familial ruptures caused by immigrating."
—*BuzzFeed*

"Profound [and] consistently refreshing . . . Wang offers candid explorations of family dynamics. . . . A tender and enduring portrayal of the difficulties of forging one's own path after spending a life between cultures." —*Publishers Weekly*

"This novel made me laugh, think, feel a bunch of things, laugh some more. And then, when I was least expecting, it snuck up and kicked me in the gut so hard I cried. Joan's voice and worldview are hard to shake, and Weike Wang's writing is immensely rewarding and enjoyable. I really, really didn't want this book to end."

—Charles Yu, National Book Award–winning author of *Interior Chinatown*

"Plucky, mordant, unflappable, the 'doctor daughter' of Chinese parents, Joan resists the American lures of affluence, consumer aesthetics, and sitcom romance. *Joan Is Okay* charts the internal story of the mythic immigrant success narrative in a tragicomedy about the costs of generational betterment."

—Mona Simpson, author of *My Hollywood* and *Casebook*

"I loved this book, once I could finally read it: The rest of my family took turns stealing it off my desk, cackling with glee, debating which characters were their favorites. This is an Asian-American novel like no other, set in the heart of the pandemic, in the city I call home. Joan is my hero."

—Ed Park, author of *Personal Days*

"This brilliant, precise, and often excruciatingly funny novel captures a truly unique heroine of the new American era, whose steadfast refusal to succumb to cliched cultural norms wins your deepest admiration, at the same time as her emotional vulnerability breaks your heart."

—Lara Vapnyar, author of *Divide Me By Zero*

"I am staggered by Weike Wang's humor, heart, and brilliance. I loved Joan and I am pressing this book into your hands."

—Lily King, author of *Writers and Lovers*

"Joan is a character I will be thinking about for a long time to come. Her extreme naivete, her lack of filter, her drive—in some ways, she's the opposite of the protagonist in Weike Wang's debut novel, *Chemistry* (one of my favorite books ever!) but they share a similar core in many ways, shaped by their similar childhoods with parents who longed to return to China, even if that meant being away from their own children. The spare, staccato prose works to accentuate the characterization to great effect. I could not put this book down."

—Angie Kim, author of *Miracle Creek*

"*Joan Is Okay* offers no easy solution or false cheer for troubling times. Rather, Weike Wang takes us into the heart of the matter: death, dysfunction, COVID, xenophobia, misogyny, and the chronic misapprehension that passes between people of good intentions. The miracle that emerges, then, is just how funny this book is, how compassionate and visionary."

—Joshua Ferris, author of *A Calling for Charlie Barnes*

"With gimlet-eyed observation and laced with darkly biting wit, *Joan Is Okay* is a deeply felt portrait of a woman who's effaced herself to survive—and how, in the face of devastating loss, she's forced to confront her grief and her place in the world. In her second novel, Weike Wang masterfully probes the existential uncertainty of being other in America."

—Celeste Ng, *New York Times* bestselling author of *Little Fires Everywhere*

"*Joan Is Okay* is a scathingly witty primer on how and how not to manage the impossibilities of either practicing medicine or being an immigrant in America, as well as a moving evocation of the kinds of both isolation and solace inherent in being a workaholic. Weike Wang is wonderful at understated sadness presented without a twinge of self-pity."

—Jim Shepard, author of *The Book of Aron*

"An engrossing and disarming novel. Joan is fine—self-contained and smart. The problem is other people. I loved this book and didn't want it to end."

—Marcy Dermansky, author of *Very Nice*

"Joan is the perfect guide for our troubled times. She interprets American culture and immigrant life with rare wisdom and laugh-out-loud humor. I was left circling sentence after sentence. Wang's writing glows, and offers readers profound and perceptive insights about how we define home, health, work, and family."     —Heidi Pitlor, author of *Impersonation*

"Joan isn't just okay, she's wonderful. I could listen to her smart, witty voice forever. Incisive yet tender, written with elegant style and delicious comic verve, Wang's story of the day-to-day life of a gifted young Chinese-American ICU doctor amply fulfills the outstanding promise of her debut novel."

—Sigrid Nunez, National Book Award–winning author of *The Friend*

"I would read anything Weike Wang writes, even a cereal box. With skillful and singular insight, humor, and heart, in her new novel Wang navigates impossible-to-talk-about territory: grief, family, the straddling of two cultures. *Joan Is Okay,* like Joan herself, is brilliant, subtly powerful, and different—in the best way."

—Rachel Khong, author of *Goodbye, Vitamin*

"Written in a distinct, original style, this story is subtle, nuanced, intense. It shows the complicated facets of the immigrant experience and speaks to many current immigrants' condition. Unflinchingly, *Joan Is Okay* challenges some of our fundamental views on home, belonging, family. A smart, quietly engaging novel that is also warm and moving."

—Ha Jin, National Book Award–winning author of *Waiting*

"Full of sly wit, off-kilter observations, and misanthropic poetry, *Joan Is Okay* introduces us to an unforgettable woman uninterested in the conventions pushed on her—by family, co-workers, and neighbors. So Joan forges her own path, one that may seem avoidant, workaholic, and even dangerous on the surface, but ultimately proves to be a testament to her idiosyncratic spirit in the face of life-changing grief. Wang asks us to reconsider our definitions of home and work, and examine our desire to label certain lives as 'healthy' and others 'unwell.' This is a novel for fans of Sayaka Murata's *Convenience Store Woman,* and Wang's own award-winning *Chemistry*. Readers will find in Joan a kindred soul."

—Lillian Li, author of *Number One Chinese Restaurant*

BY WEIKE WANG

JOAN IS OKAY

CHEMISTRY

RANDOM HOUSE

NEW YORK

IS

JOAN
OKAY

A NOVEL

WEIKE WANG

2023 Random House Trade Paperback Edition

Published in the United States by Random House, an imprint and division of Penguin Random House LLC, New York.

RANDOM HOUSE and the HOUSE colophon are registered trademarks of Penguin Random House LLC.
RANDOM HOUSE BOOK CLUB and colophon are trademarks of Penguin Random House LLC.

Originally published in hardcover in the United States by Random House, an imprint and division of Penguin Random House LLC, in 2022.

Library of Congress Cataloguing-in-Publicaion Data
Names: Wang, Weike, author.
Title: Joan is okay: a novel / Weike Wang.
Description: First edition. | New York: Random House, [2022]
Identifiers: LCCN 2021014473 (print) | LCCN 2021014474 (ebook) |
ISBN 9780525563952 (paperback) | ISBN 9780525654841 (ebook)
Classification: LCC PS3623.A4585 J63 2022 (print) | LCC PS3623.A4585 (ebook) |
DDC 813/.6—dc23
LC record available at https://lccn.loc.gov/2021014473
LC ebook record available at https://lccn.loc.gov/2021014474
International edition ISBN 978-0-593-44676-8

Printed in the United States of America on acid-free paper

randomhousebooks.com
randomhousebookclub.com

2 4 6 8 9 7 5 3

Book design by Debbie Glasserman

In the time of Hippocrates and Galen, the human body was said to have four humors, of which blood was deemed the most dominant. An excess of humor was thought to cause poor health, thus giving great importance to the practice of bloodletting.

WHEN I THINK ABOUT PEOPLE, I think about space, how much space a person takes up and how much use that person provides. I am just under five feet tall and just under a hundred pounds. Briefly I thought I would exceed five feet, and while that would've been fine, I also didn't need the extra height. To stay just under something gives me a sense of comfort, as when it rains and I can open an umbrella over my head.

Today someone said that I looked like a mouse. Five six and 290 pounds, he, in a backless gown with nonslip tube socks, said that my looking like a mouse made him wary. He asked how old I was. What schools had I gone to, and were they prestigious? Then where were my degrees from these prestigious schools?

My degrees are large and framed, I said. I don't carry them around.

While not a mouse, I do have prosaic features. My eyes, hooded and lashless. I have very thin eyebrows.

I told the man that he could try another hospital or come back at another time. But high chance that I would still be here and he would still think that I looked like a mouse.

I read somewhere that empathy is repeating the last three words of a sentence and nodding your head.

My twenties were spent in school, and a girl in her twenties is said to be in her prime. After that decade, all is lost. They must mean looks, because what could a female brain be worth, and how long could one last?

Being in school often felt like a race. I was told to grab time and if I didn't—that is, reach out the window and pull time in like a messenger dove—someone else in another car would. The road was full of cars, limousines, and Priuses, but there were a limited number of doves. With this image in mind, I can no longer ride in a vehicle with the windows down. Inevitably I will look for the dove and offer my hand out to be cut off.

—

MY FATHER'S STROKE WAS fatal, having followed the natural course of a stroke of that magnitude to its predictable end. Usually people die from complications and I was grateful he hadn't. Complications would've angered him, actually, to have died not from a single blow but from a total system shutdown, which was slower, more painful, and revealed just how vulnerable a person could be. Months prior, he had complained of headaches and eye pressure. I told him to get some tests done and he said that he would, which meant he wouldn't. In China, my father ran a construction company that, in the last decade, had finally seen success. He was a typical workaholic and for most of my childhood, adolescence, adulthood, not often around.

When I got the news, I was in my office at the hospital, at work. My father had tripped over a bundle of projector cords during a meeting and bounced his head off a chair. As my mother was explaining—either the fall triggered the stroke or the stroke triggered the fall—I asked her to put the phone next to his ear. He was already unconscious, but hearing is the last sense to go. Given the time difference on my side, only morning in Manhattan since I was twelve hours behind, my father was still en route to the meeting that by my mother's accounts was meant to be ordinary.

I asked my father how his drive was going and if he could, just for today, take a few hours off. He obviously didn't reply, but I said either way this went, I was proud of him. He had never planned to retire and remained, until the very end, doing what he loved.

*Chuàng,* I said into the phone, and raised my fist into the air.

After my mother hung up, I sat there for a while, not facing the computer, and that was my mistake.

Having seen my fist go up, the two other doctors in the office asked whom I'd been talking to and what was that strange sound I just made. I said my father and that the sound was closer to a word but the word meant nothing.

My colleagues didn't know I spoke Chinese, and I wanted to keep it that way to avoid any confusion. But the word did mean something, it had many different definitions, one of which was "to begin."

It was late September, and my female colleague Madeline was teasing my male colleague Reese about summer, which was his favorite season so he was sad to see it go.

Only little girls like summers, Madeline said to Reese, little girls in flower crowns and paisley dresses.

Reese was a six-two, 190-pound all-American guy who went on casual dates with lots of women but flirted with only Madeline at work. I'm madly in love with you, he would say to her, in front of other colleagues like me, and Madeline would either ignore him completely or relentlessly try to get him back. Madeline was a five-seven, 139-pound robust German woman with a slight accent. She has had the same software engineer boyfriend for seven years, and they lived in an apartment with lots of plants.

What's wrong? Madeline asked, sensing that I had been turned away from my monitor for too long.

I asked if one of them could cover my weekend shift. I apologized for the short notice, but I had to leave.

Both were happy to do it and even commended my request, since like my father I was a workaholic and known to never take time off. They asked where I was going and I said China, but just for the weekend. Then I turned from them and started packing up my things.

Fine, don't tell us, said Reese.

I know what it is, Madeline said with a mischievous glint. You're off to get married. You're going to elope.

*Elope* is a funny word and, in hospital-speak for patients, meant "to leave the building at the risk of yourself and without a doctor's consent."

After I mentioned my father's passing, Madeline gasped, covering her mouth and, for a second, shutting her eyes. Through her fingers, she asked if that had been my last conversation with him, and the sound I made, was it, then, a sound of grief?

I said, No, not really, and left it at that.

Reese and Madeline asked me a few more questions, like when I last saw him, and how long has it been since I left China?

You were born there, no? Reese asked, and I said I was born in the Bay Area.

California, Madeline said. A great place to be born.

But Oakland, I said, to not seem like I was giving my birthplace too much credit.

Right, Reese said.

Still, Madeline said.

I told them that the last time I saw my father was in spring. He had been in New York for business, a possible opportunity here, a new client, and, on his way back to JFK, drove past the hospital and met me in its first-floor atrium that had fake greenery and a small café. He bought me a cup of coffee and I was almost done with it when he had to leave and catch his flight. But to China, I rarely went, nor did I consider myself too Chinese.

The moment those words left my mouth, I wondered why I had said them. What was wrong with being too Chinese? Yet it'd always seemed that something was.

I felt a draft but that was impossible. Our shared office was a windowless room with a dozen desks lined up against the walls and a refreshments station in the back. The door opened to a hall that had no open windows and was used only to transport equipment. A folded-up wheelchair, an empty bed, pushed by hunched-over techs.

Madeline asked if I wanted some gum and it seemed we all

did, so we passed the gum packet around and discussed the fresh minty flavor. She asked if I wanted the rest of the pack, international flights were long. How long exactly?

I said sixteen hours, to which Reese replied shit.

I was surprised that neither asked where in China I was going. The country was huge and much of it rural. Google Maps didn't work there. But there were only two cities most people knew about, and I was going not to the capital but the other one by the sea.

———

I MET MY ONLY brother at JFK later that night. Eight years older, he was in what he called the new and fit middle age. It didn't matter to him what age I was (thirty-six)—I was younger, would always be, and he liked to tell me what to do.

Fang was rich now, his Connecticut house massive. Since he had arranged the travel, we boarded first class, where I had a small room by myself, my seat the size of a one-person L-shaped sectional, with a divider to my left that pulled open and closed. For the hour before takeoff, my brother visited me in my room to talk about how great first-class amenities were: the meals and service, different options of heated blankets, ability to re-cline and lie down, the L'Occitane bathroom kit, blue pajamas with red piping—things our father never had nor could ap-preciate.

Because he grew up in a village, I said.

It wasn't a village, Fang said. A small town in the country-side, yes, but not a village. Don't talk about things you don't understand.

Then Fang explained the L'Occitane kit. He opened his bag and held each item out between his two index fingers. This was a mini tube of toothpaste. This was a retractable comb, earplugs, moisturizer, and cologne. Tiny, powerful mints. He promised that once I flew first class, I would never be the same, there was no other way to travel.

When the meals came, we ate them in our respective rooms with silverware and drank our glass flutes of Veuve Clicquot. From across the aisle, Fang asked when I would be getting promoted at work, and I said I was already an attending/the most senior person in the room.

Sure, he said. But it can't hurt to ask, there's got to be one position higher. I said probably. He replied most definitely. Then we finished the champagne and gave back our meal trays and prepared for sleep.

But for the entirety of the flight, I didn't sleep. I didn't use the L'Occitane kit or my blue pajamas. By accident, I pushed the call button, and soon a pretty Asian flight attendant came by to ask if I needed fresh towels for my face or help with my recline. Her teeth were very white and she said that a total recline was what these chairs were built to do, to go flat like a twin-sized bed and provide passengers maximal support. Unbelievable to me that she could smile and talk at the same time, a task I once thought humanly impossible. When I didn't have a request for her, the pretty attendant reclined my sectional, pulled closed my room divider again, and dimmed the lights.

Waiting for us at Pudong airport was our mother with newly permed hair, a colorful crossbody purse, and ankles that shimmered from her translucent silk socks. My mother liked to break my name into two syllables.

Joan-na, she said, and assessed my shoulder.

During residency, I had lost the weight of a forearm. I'd since gained it back, but my mother still liked to check, and to ask if I was eating enough, if I had already eaten, if I could eat any more.

Greetings between some families can be so anticlimactic. My mother and I spoke often enough through phone calls and texts, but after two years physically apart, there were no big embraces or kisses.

She didn't greet Fang as he was already at baggage claim, ahead of the crowd. I had forgotten about crowds in China, that being in a crowd here was like being lost at sea, and for airports, train stations—for any transportation hub, any city really—for all the tourist sites, all the shopping centers, especially around the holidays, especially food markets, escalators, the phrase *rén hǎi* exists, or "people sea."

By now, Fang was twenty feet ahead of us at a sleek black booth, calling us a private sedan. In the sedan, he gave the suited-up driver with white gloves no directions. He said just the name of the hotel and the driver was off.

I was checked in with simply a handshake.

Hotel amenities: a three-inch binder.

———

A HUNDRED PEOPLE CAME to my father's funeral, most I didn't know. He had two brothers and many friends. My mother has a brother, two sisters, and more friends. These aunts and uncles I'd spent less than a week with in total for the entirety of my life.

Eighteen years ago, my parents moved back to Shanghai and have lived there ever since. Once I was bound for college, they saw their jobs as parents complete. Fang was already established then and I was on my way. None of their siblings had immigrated, and my parents were still not as comfortable in America as they'd hoped. So, after they left, it was just me and my brother in the States, the rest of our immediate family abroad.

At the funeral, I couldn't talk about my father in a significant way, and once I got a few words out others just wanted me to stop. Afterward, a smaller group of us gathered for dinner at an upscale restaurant, in a private room. The room had a round banquet table with a lazy Susan wheel built in. Customary in this country for families to sit for hours-long meals and turn this wheel back and forth, politely forcing everyone to eat. Once one meal ended, another began. Elaborate dishes were brought out, at least ten varieties of soup. Children would run around the table, laugh hysterically, and hide behind the upholstered chairs.

But there were no children at this dinner and I wondered why. To the woman next to me, I asked where so-and-so was. She pointed to herself. She was this former so-and-so, my father's youngest brother's second child, now my cousin of twenty-two.

Oh, I said.

Hasn't China changed? my cousin asked. In the last ten years, it's become brand new.

I said I didn't know the country too well.

She said that given how my face was Chinese it was a shame to know nothing about myself.

We pushed the lazy Susan clockwise and then counter-clockwise.

About our country, continued my cousin, it used to be poor, but now we have caught up. We have surpassed most Western countries, even yours.

She showed me her fancy leather wallet and told me the price. She passed me her new phone, which she noted was even more advanced than mine. So palpable to me what she was trying to prove. Everything was a race.

I told my cousin that I was sorry for her loss. My father was a good uncle to you and a good comrade overall.

———

TO RESUME WORK ON MONDAY, I had to fly back the next day. Neither Fang nor my mother suggested otherwise, as they both knew my job had come to define me and in China there was not much for me to do. My aunts had already helped my mother clean out the apartment; other family and friends regularly brought over food. My brother was also staying another two weeks to settle the rest of my father's accounts.

Fang had stronger ties to China than I did and knew more people at the funeral. Born in Shanghai, he was raised by my parents until age six and then by my mother's side—her own parents and siblings—after she and my father left for America. Common of many families at the time, that only the parents went first, and the phrase "it takes a village" has never sounded hyperbolic to me but the truth. Plan was to send for him sooner, but by accident I was born and a few more years had to pass.

From Oakland, my parents and I moved to Kansas. Then one grandparent died, followed swiftly by the other. There was a day in Wichita when I didn't know I had a sibling, and within twenty-four hours, an older brother appeared. To curious neighbors, he was simply a relative from China, visiting for a little while. Odd and obvious. A twelve-year-old boy who looked so much like my mother and half like me.

At Pudong, I went to the ticket counter to trade my first-class seat for coach. The airline clerk squinted and asked if this was what I really wanted. Once I switched to economy, I wouldn't be able to switch back. The seats in economy didn't recline into beds, I would be without L'Occitane kits and Veuve Clicquot, no more pretty flight attendant with white teeth.

Economy isn't a good time, she said in English, and if I was doing this to experience poverty or connect with the masses, it wasn't a well-conceived idea.

Clearly, she thought I was insane. While holding my blue US passport, she told her colleague beside her in Shanghainese that I probably had a disease. The colloquialism she used can be said in jest, can be well-meaning or serious. It means that something is not right about this person, that literally she has mismanaged one or two of her nerves.

The flight back was shorter, fourteen hours with a tailwind. In coach, I slept most of the way and woke up to find that I had missed both meal services included with the price. My father hated waste, so I asked the average-looking flight attendant with yellow teeth if I could have a snack.

You see, my father, I said to her, he would've been hungry, and I still need to respect his wishes.

She said not too happily that she would see what she could do.

Before landing, we hit a long stretch of turbulence that prevented anyone in coach from moving freely in the aisles. From a distance, she threw me a bag of apple slices and a shrug. The slices weren't crisp but grainy and wet. Still, I ate them all and saved the bag.

———

A COMMON CONFUSION IS between intensive and emergency care. The latter is chaotic, usually on the first floor near the ambulance drop-off, in a room without dividers or enough beds. Someone might scream, Doctor! and because no one answers, that person screams on. Intensive care is just the opposite. It's the best care that a hospital can give, and the room is quiet except for machine sounds, alarms that go on and off.

Just as radiologists know their imaging, ICU doctors know machines, ones that push oxygen into you, the all-mighty vent; ones that clean your blood, dialysis; the pumps, aka drips, that deliver medication and sedation through a central line directly to the heart. With many machines come many tubes. The endotracheal tube down the throat and to the vent for air, the nasogastric tube to the stomach for food, rectal tubes for stool, a foley for the bladder, etc. Fluid control was imperative. Too much fluid in and the body would swell. Too much fluid out and it would desiccate.

At my interview three years ago, the director asked why I chose intensive care, and I said I liked the purity of it, the total sense of control. Machines can tell you things that the people attached to them can't, I said. I liked that the sick didn't stay with us long, but for the stint that they do, we give it our all.

A sprinter, I described myself. The idea of longitudinal care wasn't for me.

My director praised my honesty and offered me the attending position right then. More so than any authority figure I'd met before, he seemed to believe in me and agreed with my point about machines. From then on I knew that we were a match.

In any specialty, an attending is expected to lead and guide her interns and residents along in their careers. To become an attending, I had trained for twelve years. The job was to teach machine readings, and a question I liked to ask was how is this patient interacting with her machine, what's the dance there like? If a patient fought, machine and patient became dyssynchronous. If they danced, the two were synchronous. Usually, the patient fought. Our innate drives to breathe and to dance alone are strong.

I taught on average three to five hours a day; the other hours were spent supervising. Procedures that I did in half the time pre-attending, I watched someone else do in double. If learning required mistakes, then teaching required watching different people make the same mistakes. Teaching was relentless déjà vu but grounding. It cemented the idea that we are all the same—height and weight did not matter, and the possibility of failure (or success) for anyone was never too far off.

To streamline the instruction process, I had a habit of printing double-sided handouts, and during morning rounds, the sound that I waited for and enjoyed most was that of my eight-person team, the pharmacist included, turning their pages in unison and on cue. The sound reminded me of the wind, which reminded me of being outside, which I currently was not.

At my first-year review, the director asked if I liked my new role here.

I said I did.

Did I respect my team?

I said I respected them on more days than not.

He commended my honesty again. Anything else he could help me with? Anything at all?

As part of my hiring package, I'd been given my own private office. But I didn't like how it echoed, or how far I had to walk from unit to office, cafeteria to office, office to another office, wasting time.

A smaller, more centrally located space comes with people, the director warned. As in you would have to share it with your colleagues, and is that what you want?

I said I would like to try.

Soon I was relocated to a shared office with other attendings. The hospital had hundreds of doctors but only ten or so for three ICUs. To my left and right sat Madeline and Reese. Before I moved in, they had heard things about me, all true.

The private office went to an older cardiologist who also wrote philosophical books about death. I tried to read one but put it down. The books were too thick, with indexes alone of a hundred pages. Death was inevitable, I didn't know what else there was to say.

—

HOW WAS CHINA? REESE asked Monday morning when I had returned. He was heading up to the surgical ICU, as I was going into cardiac. We were passing each other in the corridor meant for equipment.

I relayed my cousin's message that the country has changed. Buildings were taller and fatter, as well as the people. Obesity would soon be a problem, since food was ubiquitous, along with very high-tech phones. Everyone had a phone, and everyone paid with their phones. The economy was cashless.

But how's your family, I mean.

I asked why he wanted to know that.

You never talk about them, he said. And then this terrible thing happened. I keep wondering if you and your father were estranged. Was there a small, teensy generational or cultural gap?

To illustrate how teensy, Reese brought his pointer finger a centimeter away from his thumb.

I said my father was entirely supportive of my path.

And who wouldn't be? said Reese, standing with both hands on his waist, above the belt, in a pose that he called his "power stance." Great paths, both of us, not many people can do what we do, but put another way, what's your fondest memory of him? Your father.

I started to say something but then forgot the memory and the rest of my thoughts.

No wonder, Reese said.

No wonder what?

He didn't tell me and then quickly changed topics.

How long have you been single? he asked.

All of my life.

No boyfriends ever?

I shook my head.

Fascinating. No crushes in schools? No one-night stands in college?

I said I was busy.

But you weren't studying all the time.

In fact, I was. I asked if he thought my singleness could have something to do with my personality.

Your personality is fine.

Maybe my looks.

You're a vision.

I laughed because I knew the kind of women Reese liked: they usually had lashes. He was the vision and handsome enough to have his picture grace three of our hospital brochures for critical care. It has happened before: a family member comes in from the waiting room and flaps one of our blue leaflets around. Is this doctor in? they ask, pointing to the picture, because they want only the best, only this stately face of medicine for their unconscious and sedated loved one.

Don't take this the wrong way, Reese added, but you're a catch and you shouldn't have to look that hard. Any guy would be lucky. Not me, unfortunately, we know each other too well and I'm madly in love with Madeline. But let me know how I can help.

———

HERE WAS OUR MOTTO, as it was in any ICU: Are you suffering from ARDS, sir, madam? Because, if so, we can help.

What is ARDS?

Yes, sir, madam, we understand. Too many acronyms, not enough time.

ARDS is acute respiratory distress syndrome or severe inflammation of your lungs.

———

EACH ICU HAD PERSONALITY. The cardiac ICU had its cardiologists, lots of men coming in to talk about electrophysiology and tiny gadgets to put in the heart.

The surgical ICU had its surgeons and anesthesiologists, doctors who wrote the shortest and most indecipherable notes. The notes reminded me of haikus, and because I wasn't a literary person, I called my time in this unit difficult poetry.

The medical ICU was my favorite. With no specialties and subspecialties, it was just me and my team, meaning that I had full autonomy; I had the floor. The medical ICU saw any number of cases, and the lack of knowing what was ahead, to be in control but completely in the dark, was my jam.

This unit was also home to ECMO, or extracorporeal membrane oxygenation, or my all-time favorite machine. Four feet tall, eighty-three pounds, with tubing that could extend out farther from its body and into a person, ECMO lived only at hospitals and was worth the same amount as a luxury sedan. To keep someone alive, the machine bypassed the person's lungs and heart. Blood was pulled out of the person via a tube and funneled into ECMO to be cleaned, oxygenated, and returned. A person on ECMO could be sedated or awake. A person could walk with her ECMO as if it were a friend to lean on but also drag along. Two weeks on ECMO was average; anything longer, a month or months, was very bad news.

How could human engineers have created ECMO? I wondered. This boxy machine on a cart rarely needed maintenance, while in every public bathroom everywhere, half the automatic faucets didn't run and the only paper towel dispenser didn't dispense.

When I saw Madeline later, she was giving me notes for my rotation into medical, and I was telling her that no coincidence to me ECMO sounded similar to Elmo, that lovable red Muppet with the giant flapping mouth. I saw myself as its friend, as friend of ECMO, Tickle Me ECMO.

You need to stop anthropomorphizing, said Madeline.

It's true that I have thought of putting googly eyes on ECMO or drawing on a face.

As I was telling Madeline about googly eyes, how a set of them can make anything funny, even a blood-pumping machine, I was also eating a bagel with strawberry cream cheese. Suddenly, she leaned over into me, and I thought she had fallen or fainted, but she was trying to give me a hug. Because I wasn't near a table, it was either drop the bagel or not return the hug. I dropped the bagel, napkin, and the entire paper plate, as Madeline had never been this welcoming before.

If you ever want to talk, she said, mid-hug.

At work, Madeline was a true badass, using only her fingers to teach, no handouts, and she could run a code with impeccable form.

To run a code was to run the death algorithm, a series of

chest compressions and adrenaline shots that had a one in four chance of bringing a person back.

To call a code was to stop the death algorithm and to announce three out of four times that the person had died.

Once the hug was over, I picked up the bagel and cleaned the pink smear off the floor.

——

LIKE MACHINES, ATTENDINGS WENT on service or off, two-week intervals at a time. When they were off, you couldn't get ahold of them, you didn't know where they were. But when they were on, they were on, reachable at every second of the day, and manning their unit, unless they were asleep.

I hated being off but had two weeks of nothing at the start of October. I'd been texting with Madeline about my dilemma, that after cleaning my apartment and buying groceries, a total of two days were spent, with twelve more empty ones to go.

She asked how I felt then about having kids—that was a great way to fill time, since it was around-the-clock unpaid care.

I said my brother keeps asking me the same thing. My sister-in-law. Reese once or twice. And sometimes people I didn't really know.

A joke, Madeline clarified, from one childless woman in her thirties to another.

Two years younger than me, Madeline had just turned thirty-four. Pivotal year for women, the reproductive window coming to a close, and since she didn't know yet if kids were in her future, she had frozen ten eggs. Did you? she asked me. I hadn't. Not too late, she said. But only if I wanted to, and should she eventually decide against kids, I could have her eggs.

But then my kids might be blond, I said.

Right, she said. Kids are a risk.

I thought of how open Madeline had become after just one hug. What would happen after two?

In trying to help me fill my days, she asked about my interests, any hobbies like listening to music or reading, making art. I could visit a museum or fly to a tropical island or adopt a whole windowsill of plants.

All great ideas, but none that sparked initiative. I wasn't a creative or tropical person. Plants were hard to read and museums required too much reading.

So, what do you like?

I considered that question and finally said being on my feet for many hours at time.

Then go for a walk, she suggested. Get some exercise.

That sparked. I dressed and went out. I started circling the block in a clockwise fashion.

———

MY NEIGHBORHOOD WAS STRANGE in that it was at the intersection of three others: Harlem, Columbia University, and the Upper West Side. There was a mix of Montessori day cares and bodegas, gleaming multimillion-dollar condos two blocks away from huge brown buildings for lower-income tenants. During summer, the area was loud. People played music from their car subwoofers and set off fireworks at night. Sometimes the fireworks could sound like cherry bombs, because they were cherry bombs. And every day, a gang of motorbikes zipped by, neon yellow with purple stripes, a patriotic three-wheeler ATV in red, white, and blue. If I was home during the day, I would hear at least an hour of car horns from any of the one-way side streets clogged by a double-parked van. Occasionally there was crime, stolen packages, removed car batteries, a domestic fight dragged out into the street, drawing a crowd. Every few years, a drive-by shooting happened, targeted and aimed at one person. The death would make that evening's news and the street would be silent, only to recover the morning after.

So, the area had some danger to it, though I'd never felt unsafe. The area was also changing, with old, full residences being torn down to make room for more luxury condos and retail spots that stayed empty for months.

I walked up to the cathedral that was by the hospital and an avenue away from Morningside Park. Unfinished and one of the largest in the world, the Cathedral of Saint John the Divine had Gothic towers and arched buttresses, enormous slabs of granite and limestone, that shot up into the sky and were streaked with brown. By its main gate hung a large sign about peacocks. The church was home to three peacocks that freely explored the grounds. DO NOT FEED, said the sign in all caps. DO NOT PET.

When it started to drizzle, then pour, I turned back around.

My own residential building was distinguished-looking. A classic prewar ten-story, thirty-six-unit, and built the same year the *Titanic* sank. The entrance had an enormous black awning with ornate black crests all around. The awning was the width of the sidewalk and, from a distance, reminded me of a comically long brim on a comically tall cap. Building amenities included a twenty-four-hour doorman, and the weekday one, the head doorman, who called tenants Ms., Mrs., Mr., called me Ms. Joanna. I liked that name; I didn't mind being her. But since the day that I left for China, I felt new friction between us. In the lobby that day, he saw me with my small suitcase and said I looked particularly well. Where's the vacation? he asked. Where's the beach?

I told him about my father, which prompted him to take off his captain's hat and hold it solemnly against his chest. I'd never seen the doorman hatless and learned in that moment that he was bald.

Ms. Joanna, what a terrible thing to lose a father so young.

I said I wasn't that young.

Devastating. I'm very sorry.

I said he didn't need to apologize; how could he have known?

An awkward five minutes went by. Then my airport car came and I got in.

After my return, to avoid more awkward interactions with the doorman, I'd been entering and exiting the building through the back door with no awning. But what I had forgotten was the doorman's security camera access and his attention to details. Six four, 210 pounds, he was waiting for me in the back and stood up to acknowledge me. Polite and well spoken. But I often wished that he was polite and well spoken to someone else and I could just admire from the side.

How was your day, Ms. Joanna?

Mail came. I believe there are some things for you.

So unfortunate that you are now wet. I should have told you about the rain. I should've lent you my umbrella.

May I lend you my umbrella next time?

May I update you about thunderstorms?

May I walk you to the elevators?

He walked me to the elevators while I pressed myself against the marble wall of the lobby, wishing to be absorbed. He told me that I shouldn't do that. I shouldn't wipe myself against stone surfaces like some cleaning cloth but instead should walk with confidence and purpose.

May I push the call button for you?

May I hold open the door?

He pushed the call button for me and, when the elevator came, held open the door. I thanked him and slid into the far left corner, folding my shoulders in. He told me that that position wouldn't do. I had to stand in the middle of the elevator like the important person that I was, like men and movie stars do when they get into elevators, going up, all the way up to the penthouse suite. (Our building didn't have a penthouse; gym and laundry were on the top floor.)

I'm not that important, I said.

But you are.

I shuffled to the center and stood as straight as I could, with my shoulders back.

That's more like it, he said, and gave me a nod. Then he told me that as of today, someone has rented out 9B. I lived in 9A and 9B was the apartment across the hall that had been empty for months. Since floors six through nine had only two units each, it had just been me alone on that floor this entire time.

The doorman asked if I wanted to know more about the new renter.

I declined.

Well, he's a loquacious and helpful fellow who is about your age and doesn't seem to have a wife.

What? I said.

Congratulations, said the doorman, pushing the button for nine and releasing his hand from the door. Take care, Ms. Joanna, and best of luck.

———

THE PREVIOUS RENTERS OF 9B were a newlywed couple and their cat. The cat I never saw, but they kept saying she was around. When, one Saturday, they invited me over for dinner, I noticed that each piece of furniture was solid wood and hoisted a foot above the ground on skinny metal legs.

Clean lines, I said, and the couple introduced themselves as architects who had decorated the apartment themselves.

They were looking at me expectantly, so I said I knew nothing about feng shui. I butchered the pronunciation on purpose and said it as I'd assumed that they would to make them feel more at ease. *Fun-sway*. To sway and have fun, what a frivolous thing to do. The husband immediately corrected me.

Do you mean *fēng shui*, or wind-water, he explained quietly, since he had studied Mandarin for a semester in school. He knew a handful of characters and could write his name in Chinese with a traditional calligraphy brush.

Fantastic, I said. But what's a handful? Was that like ten? Or five? Neither will get you very far.

The husband looked at the wife, who was scrolling through her phone for something to put on.

What music do you like? she asked.

I nodded.

I meant what kind, she replied.

I said anything works, I didn't have good taste. Dinner was fast and finished in under an hour. Though I complimented their utensils, I wasn't invited back.

A year later, they had their first child, a boy, and two years later a girl. One afternoon, in passing just the wife and her new infant daughter in the hall—and having forgotten about her son—I told the wife, Girls are better to have. Girls are, on average, more punctual, organized. Girls have better handwriting, unless they become surgeons. Surgeon negates girl.

How's the cat? I would ask, until the wife finally said the cat had passed, the cat had had cancer.

Such a loss, I said, because I still hadn't met the cat and now never would.

After becoming a dad, the husband became a permanent fixture in the tenth floor laundry. But sometimes he had no laundry with him and just sat next to the washing machines, playing games on his phone. One night, the wife came to my door and asked if I had seen her husband, who seemed to be missing, and she feared something had happened to him or that he had left them. Her fingertips were trembling. She had brown stains on her shirt. I said he was probably in the laundry room shooting space zombies on his phone. Her face slackened, then hardened. How often did he do that? she asked, and I said I didn't know exactly, but he was always there when I was, always by machine seven, in a frayed, blue hoodie. She took the stairwell and ran up there, two or three steps at a time.

In the weeks before they moved out, to a New Jersey suburb, the family avoided me altogether. Whenever I entered the laundry room, the husband left even though I'd called after him in Chinese to please stay put. The wife would still say hi but simultaneously push the double stroller away. Once the stroller hit a wall, the kids cried, and the wife, for whatever reason, turned back and waved.

—

THE WIFELESS MAN OF 9B had a name, and we bumped into each other the day after the doorman had wished me luck, in the trash room of our hall, while Mark was breaking down moving boxes. Everything about him was average: five nine, 167 pounds, a face like most faces, like mine, situated somewhere between striking and hideous.

I told him that wasn't the best way to break down cardboard—he had to tear along with the grain instead of against it.

They're boxes, he said, and I said, So what if they are, boxes should be shown proper respect as well.

From then on, we kept seeing each other. In the lobby. By the mailboxes. In the hall again, while waiting for the elevator to go down at the same time.

No, you take this one, he said.

No, you, I said.

He was holding an enormous bookshelf that, as he explained, he was selling to another tenant downstairs.

I insisted he take the elevator.

Fine, I'll take it.

The shelf wasn't going to fit, and once I realized that, after watching him struggle with it—did he need help? I asked, and he said he had it, just one more push or shove, but also he was heaving and I could count every vein along his neck—I said how about I take this elevator this time, and he could take a break, drink some water, then disassemble the shelf and try again later.

He said it had fit before, when he first moved in.

I said, yes, but that was probably by a miracle and miracles don't happen twice.

Well, I'm already halfway in.

Can you get halfway out?

When I finally made it down to the lobby after that fiasco, the doorman asked if Mr. Mark and I were already in love.

I said no. I asked why.

Your cheeks are so flushed.

Not from love, I said, covering my cheeks with my hands, scraping at them to rid them of the color.

But just imagine it. Say the two of you did fall in love, then you wouldn't even need to move. A cold wintery night, he could cook for you a delicious pot of duck cassoulet and you wouldn't even need to put on a coat.

I explained that instead of love, what had flushed my cheeks was annoyance and an argument over an elevator. The doorman wagged his finger at me and warned, Don't be the prejudice. Always strive to be the bride.

—

A KNOCK. THE DOORBELL. I opened the door a sliver and saw no one there, but found a pie on my mat, along with a note from 9B that said the shelf had fit in the end, though he felt that we had gotten off on the wrong foot, so here was a chocolate pecan pie that he'd baked himself.

I took the pie in and examined it. I nibbled the crust and waited twenty minutes. Was I high? I checked my breath. Was I dead? I checked my pulse. Neither of these things, so in one night, I ate the rest of the pie. The baking tin I placed back on his mat with a note of thanks.

When we saw each other again in the hall, the mood had changed. I waited patiently as he broke down his boxes, correctly this time, and tossed out his trash.

I asked why he had so much trash. Was it a condition?

He asked why, was I a doctor?

In fact, I said.

Really?

I waited for the standard fuss over what I did for a living and the inevitable request that should he have any pains or discomfort could he come to me first? But Mark didn't do that and instead did something that made me like him more. He shrugged off my being a doctor like it was no big deal, like it was just another job, which it was. To explain the trash, he said he was an avid home cook. For baking, he could go through two dozen eggs a week. He liked to cook for other people and have low-key gatherings where everyone eats and has fun.

Our hall had started to smell nice, of something rising in the oven or simmering on the stove. Sautéed onions and tomatoes. Freshly made bread.

A knock. The doorbell. I opened the door a sliver and there he was again with another question about the building—are the water pipes always so loud? do all of your burners work?— questions that led to other questions totally unrelated to what he'd initially come to ask.

Read books? he asked.

I shook my head.

You need to read this one.

He gave the title and I nodded my head.

You've heard of it then.

I shook my head.

He wondered if we should cohost a housewarming.

I said I didn't want to do that.

Why not?

I said I didn't like parties.

Who doesn't like parties?

Me.

You? he said, then his right eye closed briefly, possibly to wink. Then he walked slowly backward, down the hall, with his face still toward me. Could be fun. Could be great. Mull it over, you.

As odd as my new neighbor was, a great thing about him was that while he was at my door, a quarter of an hour at a time, talking, he never asked me questions about myself. Whether I was married, had kids, wanted to get married, wanted to have kids, or what my life was like, he didn't seem to care. Relieved of any expectation to respond, I could simply listen and fun-sway along in my head. If my on-service brain was the trenches, then my off-service one was a meadow. If I was part trench, part meadow, then Mark was a roundabout. On and on he could go without making any real progress.

He used to be in publishing and when he said that, I said wow, publishing, except I knew no one in publishing or anything about that field.

Yeah, I used to be at a house, he said so coolly as if he had immediately expected me to be impressed.

A house? I asked. A house and not a building?

The house was in a building, two whole floors.

Oh. But I still didn't quite understand.

He said the job itself was stimulating, with lots of similar-minded people around, but corporate life stifled him, and he didn't like the feeling of being a cog.

Did or didn't? I asked, hoping I'd just misheard. Cogs were essential and an experience that anyone could enjoy.

Didn't, he enunciated. He hated that feeling. So, he'd quit last year to freelance-edit and consult from home.

Previously he had lived in the West Village, Hell's Kitchen, and the 8os of the Upper West Side, but never this far uptown. He liked to try out different neighborhoods and looked forward to what each new experience could afford. He asked for the official name of ours and I said there wasn't one, which he dismissed as couldn't be true. If you lived in as vibrant a place as this, you had to get the name right or else people would suspect that you were trying to get more street cred than you deserved.

I told him I had no street cred, so asking me about it was useless.

Yeah, but say he still wanted to discuss it, say it was our civic duty to find out. Was this area actually the Upper West Side or more specifically Manhattan Valley or Morningside Heights or SoHa?

SoHa? I asked.

Southern Harlem.

I said that was not an acronym I knew.

He complained about having too much stuff. Whenever I saw him during those initial weeks, he would wonder how through all his moves he'd managed to accumulate three copies of the same book, repeats of silverware, glassware, Dutch ovens, frying pans, reusable shopping bags, electric mixers. From here on out, a resolution. He wanted to be, or at least aspire to be, a person with fewer things.

So, outside his door, he started to leave filled boxes that by the end of the day were gone. Through my peephole, I watched other tenants come and inspect the items, then carry them away. Some even knocked on his door to chat and without exception, Mark would invite this tenant in or offer them homemade food.

For a while his resolution seemed to be working until Mark mentioned that his steep drop in stuff now bothered him and that he'd never set out to be a minimalist, after which packages started to arrive for 9B, in piles in the lobby, and whenever I saw him sign for them at the desk, he was holding large shopping bags, one under each arm.

Our ninth-floor hall had a window that was equidistant from 9A and 9B and aligned perfectly with the bathroom window of an adjacent building, less than an arm's reach away. If I opened this window, I could touch the brick of that building, I could tap on the glass. Multiple times a day, the same man on the other building's ninth floor sat in his bathroom, on the toilet, and thus in the center of both our two windows, framed by them, like an old painting. I called him Enormous Man, because even after three years, I still had no clue about his weight or height. He sat at eye level with you, motionless, his own eyes cast downward and with one sock draped over each bare shoulder.

The constant influx of new things into 9B and efflux of old things reminded me, yes, of a roundabout, but also of people who liked to eat while on the toilet, though I never saw Enormous Man eat.

———

THERE WERE TWO PIECES of mail in my box today. The first, a Shen Yun brochure in a trifecta of colors, golds, reds, and greens—absolutely the number one show in the world, a must-see. (I'd never gone to a Shen Yun show but got flyers from them all the time, along with Chinese pamphlets about Jesus and Falun Gong leaflets about the terrible evils, like organ harvesting and imprisoning, that happened every second on Chinese soil. I didn't know how these people found my address, but being on these mailing lists was an exercise in cognitive dissonance, that on one hand the four-thousand-year history of my motherland was glorious, and on the other modern China was the worst, so please turn to Jesus.)

The second piece of mail was a West Side Hospital brochure in our trademark color of calming ocean blue with a white font. West Side Hospital cares about your health, it said. Come learn more about our multidisciplinary, interdisciplinary, evidence-based, team approach to care.

But if you came, wouldn't you be sick or visiting a patient? Does anyone come to a hospital to learn more about the fortress itself?

I'd once heard an EMT liken being in an ambulance to being in a show. The lights, the sounds, and, if you do your job right, the glory.

On the brochure's front flap was the familiar picture of Reese that I had seen around the hospital, on side tables, chairs, stuffed into an acrylic holder mounted to the walls of reception rooms. Distinguished, experienced-looking, but not fatigued, with his white coat and polished stethoscope, posing with the stacks of machines beside a pristine, empty bed.

———

IT WASN'T GLORY THAT had drawn me to health care work but the chance to feel pure and complete drudgery in my pursuit of use. I had to feel totally spent after work, else I wouldn't have felt like I worked. So being in the trenches was a delight but it also meant that the sky was as pitch-black when I entered the hospital as when I left. Then in passing the grand cathedral, the facade of which was lit up by artificial lights, I would realize that I hadn't seen the sun. The sun had risen and set that day, and supposedly all the days of this week, but I hadn't thought about it once.

As the director had put it when he hired me, I was a gunner and a new breed of doctor, brilliant and potent, but with no interests outside work and sleep. I'd asked if he was trying to compliment me or insult. Compliment, he'd said. Because being a gunner was good. Disease is war, and in war, gunners operate the artillery.

For whatever reason, the director still liked to compliment me. The remarks would come on spontaneously, without warning, and the overall situation left me feeling worse, like he thought I needed the praise or else I would keel over. But did I say thank you during or you're welcome after? Did I say nothing at all and just let him carry on?

On my first Friday back on service, around 3:00 p.m., the director paid the shared office a visit when no attendings were around except me. Per protocol, attendings were summoned to see him. A director's office was much nicer, and our director in particular loathed in-between-meeting gaps.

I asked if I was in some kind of trouble.

Not trouble at all, he said, and sat perched at the edge of my desk like a professionally dressed five-six, 149-pound bird. He went on to say that my work this year had been more than satisfactory, that as with last year, I had gone above and beyond, etc.

I listened. I smiled. I felt my teeth get cold from not being able to recede back into my mouth.

When the compliments were done, he said he wanted to check in and make sure that I was okay to work and didn't need more time off.

I said I'd just finished two weeks of doing nothing.

But do you need more time?

My director had never asked me that before, so I asked if this had something to do with my father.

He had heard about my father, yes, but this had nothing, or at least very little, to do with him. If I needed more time to process, it was a complete nonissue. He could just make Doctor Baby-Blue Eyes work extra.

Doctor Baby-Blue Eyes was Reese, but we couldn't call him that in public anymore since HR had informed everyone in a training that there would be no more derogatory nicknames or ragging on other colleagues or on specialties. No more "dermatology is on dermaholiday" or "orthopedics is run by boneheads." Though the main issue I had with Reese's nickname was that he had green eyes, not blue. I reminded the director of that detail, and he joked that I was getting soft.

Not soft, I said. Accurate.

We laughed.

So, we're good? he asked.

I said indeed. At this point, I thought the director would leave, but he remained perched on my desk with a far-off look.

I followed his gaze to an empty corner of the room. I worried he was having a seizure or seeing a ghost.

Sir?

Incredible to him that I had gone to China for a weekend. There and back, in only forty-eight hours. Extraordinary, he said. But what was even harder for him to believe, and he didn't mean to offend, only to be transparent, was that though he knew me to be ethnically Chinese, he hadn't expected me to still have relatives back there, let alone a father. Further, it wasn't the sudden death that had struck him, but the thought of my having a father at all. Maybe he'd never imagined me in relation to a father, even though I obviously had one—everyone had a father, even a child with two mothers; it made perfect biological sense.

I looked back at that corner again, which was still empty, but now I worried he had seen my father's ghost and I had missed it.

This is coming out wrong, the director continued, waving a hand across his face as if to erase it.

The motion reminded me of an Etch A Sketch and how in clearing the screen you had to violently shake the apparatus of aluminum powder.

To comfort him, I said that I had the same thought all week about the sun. I had forgotten about it all week, though the world would perish without one.

Right, but fathers are quite different from suns, aren't they? Suns. Sons. Icarus should've listened to his father and not flown so close.

I didn't quite catch my director's drift and asked if he was trying to be clever. He cleared his face again and said he was just trying, unsuccessfully, to lighten the mood.

So, what was he like? Your dad.

Normal guy, I said. Nothing out of the ordinary.

My director said he'd had a look at my file.

Oh yeah?

I know your mom is still in China, but you have a brother here in the States, in Greenwich. That's not too far.

Not at all.

The two of you get along?

Very much so. I love my brother. We met in Wichita.

Met? You mean where you were born.

No, I was born in Oakland.

And him?

He would probably say Connecticut.

What's he like?

My brother? Just another average Joe.

—

THE AVERAGE JOE IN America is expected to move 11.4 times in his life. Who knows about the average Jane. From Wichita, we moved to Scranton, Pennsylvania. From Scranton to Bay City, Michigan. More town than city, Bay City was the last place we would live together as a family, and for only two years. Then counting my moves within Massachusetts, from dorm to dorm and later to New York for work, I was right under the average at eleven.

During my childhood and adolescence, we moved because of my father. His dream enterprise was in construction, like an enterprise that sold tarps, specifically the waterproof tarps used to cover unfinished sites. But wherever he tried to start this business, no bank would lend him money for it and the enterprise would fail. He could look suspicious: gaunt cheeks; extra-small, inset eyes; a few very long whiskers that sprouted out around his mouth. Whenever the business failed, he would wash his hands of the state. Time to start anew, he would say, time to break new ground.

My father was an optimist. For the number three, he would touch his index finger to his thumb, the same hand gesture as for the A-OK.

The only business routes available to him were to open a Chinese restaurant or convenience store, and neither he was interested in. There wasn't enough time (or money) to go back to school for an MBA, which was where he thought the real problem lay, not in his appearance but the lack of American degrees. He took on odd jobs, washing dishes at restaurants, delivering newspapers, landscaping, stocking store shelves, while my mother cleaned houses. Average people, my parents. Who raised two average kids.

But as average parents, they still differed in small ways. I could have told Reese this memory of my father, but he wouldn't have understood.

A Chinese saying: Hitting is love, berating is love. Had I explained that to Reese, he wouldn't have known what I meant. He would have overreacted and judged me. What kind of love is that? What kind of parents did you have?

When my father was truly angry about something, he could berate me for hours but afterward offer to buy me ice cream. My mother could berate for hours too, but no ice cream afterward, and while berating, she could multitask, she could move swiftly through a room to collect a large portion of my things. She would put my things in a plastic bag and double knot the bag. Then she would put the bag on a high shelf. In hindsight, she was trying to fortify something in me. A person shouldn't sentimentalize or believe anything to be precious. But in a month, there would be two or three bags on that shelf, and inevitably all of my things would be gone.

I hadn't been an easy child. Quiet, a recluse, and disastrously clumsy. I spilled things like cough syrup as I was taking them, the red dye flooding the dingy carpet of our rental and impossible to get out. We couldn't tell the landlord so my mother put a rug over it, after which I was berated, then had all my things put into bags.

Mostly my mother wanted to know why I couldn't be a happier child. Why are you looking at me like that? she would ask, and I hadn't looked at her in any way. But there we were in a supermarket aisle, across any table, in a car just her and me, my mother in the driver's seat, speeding past cornfields, miles of flat land, glaring not at me but the road ahead.

What look? I would ask.

That look that I owe you something, that I've wronged you in some way.

A pessimist, a constant speculator. Had she known what America was like, she might not have immigrated. Had she not been an immigrant, she might have enjoyed being a mom. Raising you took off half my life, she would say. You're living proof of where that half went.

(Chemists know this already. All elements on the periodic table decay and in one half life, half the original element, called the parent nucleus, decays into a different element, or the daughter nucleus. No son nucleus, of course. No son could ever be a by-product of radioactive decay.)

Hitting is love: The last day I was in China, I tried to give my mother a hug and she recoiled, but then she brought one hand over my shoulder and started pounding my back as if I were choking. I pounded hers in return and she continued to pound mine. We hacked a little and this went on for a few seconds. It reminded me of chest compressions, the ones that you have to do during codes. You must always stay calm. But you must also be willing to break all the person's ribs in order to keep her alive.

—

DURING MY OVERNIGHT SHIFT, a new number with a Connecticut area code texted me with the sentence, This is your mother. I ignored the text, because of so much spam these days and my mother was in China.

I was at the foot of a bed of an eighty-year-old man whom we were trying to resuscitate but who ultimately could not be. Ten years older than my father and I had watched him die because I had been watching his cardiac monitor, but with machines, there was always a paradox, if I'd been watching this monitor, had I really seen him die? Afterward, I did the death exam. Check the eyelids and the pulse, close the jaw. No one cried. The family wasn't here. Then I sat down in the nurses' bay, at one of their computers, to note the time of death and to start the postmortem care. The body had to be bagged and taken away, the area disinfected and remade for the next person. During this lull, my phone rang again with the same number and I picked up. It was 2:00 a.m.

This is your mother, said a voice that sounded a lot like hers. It's late but I need someone to talk to. I'm having terrible jet lag.

My mind made the quick switch out of hospital mode and into real life. It was as simple as switching languages, from English to Chinese, the latter in which my parents and I had always communicated.

But your number, I said. It says you're calling from Connecticut.

Which is where I am. Why else would I have jet lag?

Greenwich? You're currently in Greenwich, Connecticut?

Am I cutting out or something? she asked. Am I not coming through clear enough?

Very clear, I said.

Your brother. He coerced me. He dangled plane tickets in front of my face.

I asked a few more questions. When did she get in? Why had no one told me? How long was she staying? The winter? She was here to spend the rest of winter? Why had she not told me? How did she know that I was awake?

I'm telling you right now, she said. And you are awake, aren't you?

The other questions she dismissed as logistics, for me to confirm with someone else, like Fang. She just needed someone to chat with, complaining that everyone in Connecticut, everyone in this small tiny state, was asleep.

To chat is to *liáo tiān,* or literally "to gab about the sky." For the past eighteen years, calls with my mother were purely information driven, and even when we lived in the same house, it was not like her to find me just to chat.

If you don't chat with anyone, Mom, if you just lie perfectly still, then you'll fall asleep.

No, I won't. And I'm not tired, she said. She announced that she would kick off our *liáo tiān* with a slew of nice things. All children like to hear nice things and all adults are children at heart.

Joan-na, I would've moved in with you, but you don't have any kids. I would've chatted with you before, but I didn't want to waste your time. More mothers should learn to let go, and what I hoped for you was a busy life. Now that you have that and a successful career, you should thank me for being your mother and not a burden on your life.

After I thanked her, she said that I'd matured, a second nice thing. Parents run out of steam, immigrant parents especially, and once Fang had met all her expectations, she feared that I, being second born, would be the one to rebel. Horror stories. The youngest child squanders her chances to become an entitled brat and to gnaw on the bones of the old, which was the literal phrase. But thank God you didn't become one of those and now make your own money. A woman must make her own money, because without money there is no power, and a woman must have power.

I looked at the clock on my monitor. It was 2:23 a.m. Then 2:24 a.m.

She asked if I had heard her.

I said that I had. But she had told me all this before.

When?

For as long as I could remember, all through childhood, really. Her fear that I would not mature paired with her hope that I would someday have power. Because she didn't have any power and being an immigrant mother was a half-life.

Forget I said those things, my mother now said. They were said in times of duress, you have to understand. Moving forward, I'd like to be there for you, more especially since I'm here, so feel free to call me anytime, even if I don't pick up. Leave a message is what I mean and I'll get back to you within the hour. All in all, I'm grateful for you so let's continue to engage.

I didn't know my mother could talk like this and assumed that it was related to my father.

I asked her if she was grieving.

Am I grieving? Is that really the question you're asking?

I said it was just a question. Grieving was a necessary process and there were many waiting-room brochures about it.

She told me that I needed to work on my *liáo tiān* skills.

What are you doing tomorrow? I asked.

Seeing the rest of your brother's house. She yawned and I told her to go back to bed.

She said she couldn't until we'd hung up and she couldn't hang up until I did. In order to provide more support, she'd promised herself to stop hanging up on her kids. So, if I could hang up, that would be ideal.

But I don't want to hang up either. It's not very filial.

You have my permission.

I can't, I said, worried that my hand would immediately fall off after I put the phone down.

Why would that happen to your hand, Joan-na? Are you the undead?

Humor was a coping mechanism, said the brochures, but they never mentioned how long after a death in the family was it appropriate to start using the word *dead*. When I still couldn't hang up on my mother, she told me to count to three with her and at three, we ended the call at the same time.

Afterward, the nurse next to me, who had been sitting next to me the whole time, said that she didn't know that I spoke Chinese. I apologized out of reflex and when she looked confused, I apologized for confusing her.

No, it's cool that you do, she said.

There were times my classmates would ask me to translate some dumb English phrase into Chinese just to prove to them that I could, then after hearing me speak Chinese, just to say that I sounded foreign.

I waited for the nurse to do that, but of course she didn't, since she was a good person and a good nurse, and we were both adults.

—

MY MOTHER'S WORRIES HADN'T been unfounded. As a child, I was at medium to high risk of not maturing—many trips to the counselor's office, a persistent lack of friends.

My first counselor in Scranton asked if I had thoughts of hurting myself. You do not smile, she said, and if you do not smile, how is anyone going to know what's going on in that big head?

The Joker smiles a lot, I replied.

The Joker isn't real, she said.

That I often answered questions strangely was a reason I was sent to her office in the first place.

Concerns, concerning, and teachers wrote in my report cards that while my academic performance was excellent, they didn't know much about me, and my personality was a mystery. Compared with other kids, I was too quiet and shy. Why didn't I ever speak up? Or participate in group discussion? Or have anything else to add?

Because I had only a limited amount to say. Better to distill our words down to a single point, I thought, hence why I've always admired bullet-pointed handouts and needles.

But when I said that last part about needles, a second counselor thought I was using recreational drugs. He began to call out specific drugs, asking which ones I'd used, an entire alphabet I was unaware of. I could only say that his list would make a great children's book, cautionary but educational.

Counselor Three of Bay City suspected that I would find myself later. College was the best years of my life, he said. He had joined a fraternity and met his wife. These things can happen to you too. But a sorority, he clarified, and a husband.

Counselor Three's office was covered with insignias of our state school, his alma mater. The insignia was a green helmet, like the kind worn during battle in ancient Greece. Our state school was behind in academic anything but was sports champion every year. Counselor Three played no sports though continued to be an overzealous fan.

About the sorority and husband, I said, I'll have to see. But as my brother had, so would I choose a fancy college far away from where I had been raised and in a state that I'd never lived.

At eighteen, I was dropped off at Harvard, and within a few months my parents had sold most of their things and left the country. The speed and style of their exit would remind me of those old cartoons, the final line. That's all, folks!

I had been prepared, told on and off again that eventually my brother and I would have to look after each other and be on our own. But was I a child of immigrants anymore, if technically they had returned?

Back in Shanghai, my parents would finally become upper middle class. All of China was rebuilding and all of China needed waterproof tarp. When my father visited me last spring, he said that the next time he was in town, which he hoped would be soon should this new client go through, he would allot more time for me and even park his rental car. In spring, he hadn't parked. Hospital parking was $17.99 an hour, and if he couldn't stay the entire hour, then the price per minute was exorbitant. So, he left his rental car running with its flashers on and in direct line of sight from the atrium table where we sat.

Do you need money? he asked, and I said I didn't, but still he pushed a crisp, brand-new one-hundred-dollar bill into my hand. Next time you'll tell me all about it, he said. The *it* could be whatever—your day, your work, your life. Just as when I was in college and would get a two-minute phone call from him, from a train or airplane gate where he was about to board—next time you'll tell me all about college, and I'll tell you all about my trip.

Not much about college to tell. Harvard was intense but some parts were fun. Each spring there were outdoor concerts and barbecues. A large banquet table ran down the entire length of the yard and was filled with hot dogs and every kind of condiment. Each fall there were football games, one in particular against a rival school in not-so-far-from-Greenwich, Connecticut, with which we had a history. My brother had gone to Yale, and for months prior to the big game, each year, he would ask if I wanted to come. He and his alumni finance friends had bought out two rows of VIP seats and all-new school gear.

Did I go?

No, never. As neither team was good, the tailgate started at 7:00 a.m., and I could study more or less around the clock. I went from library to classroom and only returned to the dorm to sleep. I wasn't close with any of my roommates, and once the rest of them decided to be in a suite, I became a floater.

Studying so much had its consequences. It caused me to wonder, for instance, if I might be a genius. Prior to medicine, I'd entertained the idea of going into higher math, which was math above the boring numbers and calculations. Higher math did away with all that, was purely symbols and proofs and style. Proofs were like puzzles. But a simple one-page proof took me nearly a week to understand. I wasn't a genius in the end, but a girl could still hope.

Better not to be one, said my brother, who was much more gifted in math and could've gone into higher math had he not so badly wanted to be rich. Sure, some geniuses solve the unsolvable problems and win unwinnable prizes, but they still forage for mushrooms for the rest of their days.

My brother had a point. It was much nicer and safer to buy mushrooms from a store.

Fang was what future employers would call a "diamond in the rough," possessing true grit but also someone whom they knew they could groom.

I was what some would call properly "lopsided," or the opposite of well rounded, and being a girl lopsided in science and math was supposedly good.

My childhood dreams consisted of stone castles made only out of turrets and colorful fluttering flags, me flying high above them, over moats and green pastures filled with white specks of sheep. Once I finished college and the yearlong marches through physics, chemistry, biology, and math, these dreams stopped. Then, as new doctors, we were warned that medical training would flatten us. The learning curve was relentless, akin to drinking from a fire hydrant or the fattening of ducks to make foie gras. I'd never tasted foie gras before nor did I want to be a duck, so the open fire hydrant analogy it was. A person sits eye level with the barrel and grapples it. She is pounded in the face by knowledge while her facial features are erased.

—

AT THE END OF my shift, I went back to my apartment to shower and then left immediately, hair still wet, for the Harlem–125th Street Metro-North station. I boarded the train to Stamford by 9:15 a.m. and, within the hour, was in Greenwich, Connecticut. Even without the sign, I knew I'd arrived. The ground was free of litter. The air felt clean against my skin. Trash bins were painted hunter green. I was hungry, but outside the station, instead of hot dog stands and halal carts, there were only car dealerships. I could buy a new BMW or Lexus. I could visit a billion-dollar hedge fund.

Weekday afternoons, Fang worked inside one of these funds, the boys were each in private school, and Tami was out. My sister-in-law no longer worked but had become actively involved in school events and weekly appointments for self-care. Fang and Tami also enjoyed hosting and had three big holiday parties a year, the first of which set around Thanksgiving.

I'd told neither of them that I was coming that morning because I didn't want my brother to take the rest of his day off so he could pick me up, then drive me around Greenwich for what would become an hour-long tour. Belle Haven. The waterfront. The new Tesla store. Can't you see yourself thriving here? he would ask. Can't you see yourself in a Tesla? He was on a waiting list for the next model, and because of that, we had test-driven one together during my last Greenwich tour. I found it too quiet, so quiet that I wondered the entire time if the engine had dropped out the vehicle and effectively its bottom. So, was driving a Tesla like hitting rock bottom?

Catastrophizing. Thinking about disastrous possibilities

based on a relatively small observation or event can lead to believing that the worst-case scenario is the one that will play out.

If they knew I was here, Tami would bring the boys home early from school and request an elaborate meal from their chef. I would be asked to stay the night. Because if I came, then I couldn't not stay the night. I would have to stay and discuss with Tami and Fang my future plans. Why not start a private practice in Greenwich? they'd ask. Doctors around here had two, three practices each. Greenwich was the second-safest town in Connecticut, with a safety index of 0.9 out of 1 (the state itself hovered at 0.77). Whereas my zip code's index was 0.46 or an F or an automatic fail. In China, cities are much safer than the suburbs, the U.S. is just the reverse. You know this, Jiu-an, Fang would say, Jiu-an being my Chinese name and also the Chinese-ification of Joan. You know this, so he didn't understand my choice to knowingly live in an unsafe place. What didn't I like about suburban life? What did I have against trees and more space? Suburbs represent family, and the heart of America lives here.

Only around my family did I catastrophize. I never did it at work. I never saw a pimple and thought death in two and a half days. Even though a hospital was where something like that could be true.

From Greenwich station, I called a cab.

My brother's ten-acre compound was made up of a main house, a guesthouse, and a four-car garage. The main house was just over six thousand square feet. It had six beds, six baths, an imperial staircase, vaulted ceilings, an indoor/outdoor pool with a sauna. The guesthouse had two bedrooms, two baths, and a garden-facing kitchen. The grounds had perennial gardens, a tennis court, a basketball court, an antique stone wall, a bridge that went over an artificial pond filled occasionally with koi, winding footpaths, and a verdant lawn for limitless summer fun. The nearest neighbor was across the street but also two acres away, from my brother's very long driveway and up the neighbor's.

The last time I'd visited was at the start of last summer, three months before our father passed away. After we test-drove the Tesla, Fang and I came back to the compound and Tami joined us out in the yard, under a wood cabana, by their perennial gardens. I could hear my nephews screaming from somewhere on the property but I couldn't see them. Their screams of fun were indistinguishable from those of pain and reminded me of emergency rooms. I inspected my fingernails and then the lawn, a continuous carpet of green. I asked Fang how often they cut the grass and it was more often than my nails.

But we don't have to cut anything ourselves, Tami said from behind a pair of sunglasses. We have people to do that.

Now the lawn was a little less green and the trees had changed colors.

The cabdriver looked up at the gables of the main house as he drove. He said, You live here, miss?

I said, Oh no, I'm just on staff.

Then I was at the front door knocking and ringing the bell for what would become a full fifteen minutes until their housekeeper let me in. The housekeeper was different from the property manager, who was different from the groundskeeper.

In truth, I never knew exactly how many staff members at any given time were on the premises.

Where is she? I asked, and the housekeeper offered first to take my coat. I said I could hold it; I wasn't staying for very long. Then she led me to a woman I hardly recognized, sitting in a corner of one of their foyer rooms that functioned as an antechamber for those who'd just arrived. My mother was thinner. Her cheeks had hollowed in and there were so many lines around her face that hadn't been there before. I asked if she'd fully unpacked, and of course she had; the moment she arrived, the housekeeper had taken her three suitcases, one by one, upstairs. Each garment was pressed and hung up. The thermostat in my mother's bedroom set to the cool 68°F temperature that she liked.

The house is too big, my mother said from the foyer. I didn't know where to start.

I suggested the kitchen, and we made our way there, where I put on a kettle of water. Hot water was a Chinese staple. Even I drank mugs of it year-round out of habit and now comfort. My parents could never get used to the amount of cold water everyone drank in America or understand why even historically hot beverages, like coffee and tea, had to be iced. For our mother's arrival, my brother had bought several electric kettles and placed them around the house. There was one in her bedroom, so at night she wouldn't need to come downstairs in the dark. Considerate, but I was also reminded of a former patient who had checked himself in for shortness of breath. He was my father's age, but the similarities stopped there. White and wide. Even with an oxygen mask on, he had no problem telling the intern about the ongoing renovations of his new East Hampton home. Going well, he said unironically. My wife wants a treadmill in every room, so she doesn't have to exercise in one place.

I asked if my mother had noticed all the water kettles. How through this, Fang was at least trying to make her feel more at home.

At home I have only one kettle, she said. And it's not fancy like these, it's very plain and old. Your baba boiled all of our water.

We sat side by side on the barstools, along the massive kitchen island. My mother held the hot water mug to her face and blew steam off its surface like smoke.

I asked if she could do me a favor.

She took a slow sip.

Could she not tell the others about my coming here today?

She took a slower sip.

I'm serious, I said. Because she and Fang were the casebook mother-son pair. They spoke to each other about all and rarely fought.

Who am I going to tell? she said. Your business is your own. She wasn't going to get involved.

When the hot water was finished, an hour had passed and it was time for me to leave. I got into another cab back to the station, and this cabdriver asked the same thing: You live back there, miss?

I said my mother did for now.

So, where to? he said, as we went down the driveway and onto the road.

I didn't answer him.

Spa? Country club? Where we going, miss?

I didn't answer him.

He pulled over to the shoulder after a red light and stopped the cab.

She doing all right? Your mother?

I said I didn't know yet, it was too early to tell.

Just her in that big house then?

No, I said. My brother lives there too, my sister-in-law, three boys under ten, a rotating staff.

But my father, I said, and after those words, I had to look out the window.

I can understand that, the cabdriver said, and turned his blinkers on. Just let me know when you're ready.

Twenty minutes later I said he could take me to the station.

—

THERE IS NO REAL fight against death because death will always win. But death can be handled well or poorly.

The first death I saw happened when I was a child. My mother, who had been holding my hand, stopped holding my hand to scoop me up and to turn me away. But I had seen it. A hit-and-run. The man's body facedown on the side of the street, with blood pooling at the elbows and knees; the skin ballooned outward, blue and thin, like plastic bags about to burst. A death handled poorly.

My father's death had been handled well. In China, I had reviewed all his charts, alongside a translator, from routine checkups in his last decade to the adverse event itself, and deemed the stroke properly managed, with the right meds given and the right algorithms performed. Disease can have no reasoning to it, coming down to either bad genes or bad luck or a combination of both. Every death was sad, but in a hospital at least there was a process around it, a box, and once that process was clear, death, while always the victor, could be contained.

———

ONE LARGE PIECE OF mail that did not fit inside my box was left on the floor beneath.

A thick silken envelope, color burnt orange, or rust, or autumn maple, with my name written in cursive and green foil lettering. The envelope came attached to a wicker basket.

I was cordially invited, at the end of the month, to Fang and Tami's annual Harvest Bash. Activities would include an on-site horse-drawn hayride, a petting zoo (goats, peacocks, and mini horses), face painting (back by popular demand), and make your own cornucopias. Come taste our handcrafted seasonally spiced cocktails, the invite said. RSVP required two weeks in advance.

Last year's Harvest Bash didn't have a petting zoo.

I imagined someone with a peppermill cracking fresh flakes into every drink.

The basket came with one pound of Royal Riviera pears, two pounds of seasonal apples, six ounces of gouda cheese, four ounces of cheddar cheese, a cranberry orange loaf cake, a pumpkin spice loaf cake, trays of assorted nuts (pecans, roasted almonds, honey roasted cashews), one pound of cranberry pear chutney, one pound of caramel sauce.

Goats had rectangular pupils, I knew, and sometimes screamed like humans. But did they care for cranberry pear chutney? Or caramel sauce?

I didn't know what to do with the sauces. The Royal Riviera pears I gave to my doorman, cheeses and nuts to Mark. Loaf cakes I could eat and in two nights they would be gone.

The day it arrived, Fang texted to ask if I'd received a basket.

I texted back that the basket was safe and mostly consumed.

Good, he wrote. Then he asked for my RSVP to the bash.

Right now? I wrote back.

Cool, he replied. I'll put you down for two. Bring a friend. Anyone you like.

———

I HAD NO WALL decor in my living room except for a giant wall calendar about half my height, with just the grid of the dates, all lines and numbers, no pictures. When the month was over, I ripped the half-body sheet clean off and, more than the breeze from my handouts, the calendar produced a gust.

Overheard in the elevator, between a young couple going up to the ninth floor with me. Same weight and height, this couple, woman and man both 143 pounds, five six and a half, and I wondered if this commonality had brought them together.

Books, the man was saying to the woman, 9B consults on books and culture. He tells you what you could write about and how you should think about yourself in this cultural moment.

What cultural moment? I asked, and the couple turned around. I said I lived in 9A but had nothing to do with 9B, I was just eavesdropping, just curious.

Curiosity killed the cat, said the woman.

Actually, it was cancer, I said, thinking of the former cat of 9B.

The man looked at the woman and vice versa. They both turned from me and we got out on the same floor, but diverged.

He did recommend a lot of titles to me. One evening, he dropped off a stack of books that he had multiple copies of but couldn't bear to just donate. Books that he'd read in school that had been helpful and enriching at the time. Not necessarily his favorites, but classics that everyone should read. The bag was bulky, and he went through each title with me at my doorway, starting with Steinbeck's *The Grapes of Wrath*.

I turned the book over and read the description: a naturalistic epic, captivity narrative, road novel, transcendental gospel about the Great Depression.

Whose grapes again? I asked.

No, the author's name is Steinbeck. John Steinbeck.

When I stared blankly back at him, he ran a hand frantically through his hair.

Dozens of books in the bag, some thick, some thin. I tried to pretend that I knew most of them. Oh yes, that one, I would say, pointing, when the last humanities class I took in college was the last time I had to read a book that did not contain only facts.

A page a day, Mark suggested. But well worth it. That was how he finally made it through Proust, he said.

And I said, Me too.

Besides books, he had many thoughts about the city and the kind of person who chose to live here. New York was a true melting pot, but what made a true New Yorker was this or that, a unified belief system of tolerance, of live and let live, that couldn't be replicated anywhere else. New Yorkers weren't rude, they were brusque, witty, sharp; they told you exactly what they meant, no bullshit or fake pleasantries. From here, somehow, we wound our way to the Yankees. Every New Yorker has an opinion about them, so what was mine?

I asked if he was talking to me about baseball.

Baseball? he said and kept tucking brown locks behind his ear. They didn't look bad there nor did they undercut anything he'd just said. Brown with streaks of chestnut, thick and slightly wavy, no frizz. By a certain age I was told to stop playing with my hair in public and especially while I spoke. You don't want to grow up into one of those, do you? a teacher or other adult would ask. A woman who twirls her hair while speaking is a woman never to be taken seriously.

What other sport is worth watching and discussing? he continued in a deeper, more somber voice. Football is too militant. The gridiron, the idea of gaining yardage and gaining ground. Baseball is in every way more perfect; there are no flaws in the game, hence why it's America's sport and pastime. Just consider how pastoral baseball is. It's all about going home.

Huh, I said, because I'd never thought about baseball like that nor had anything profound to say about sports. Did a person then need to watch baseball to have America be her home? Neither of my parents had watched any and neither considered this country home.

That I didn't have a television also surprised him.

You don't have a TV? But how do you watch . . . He listed out the things I was supposed to have watched from both past and present. I was missing out on the ubiquity of NY1 news, game shows like *Jeopardy!*, famous movies set in this city (where to even start? he said), and famous sitcoms (only one place to start). The show about nothing. Jerry and Kramer, two neighbors who live across the hall from each other, like he and I, long-term pals who get into all sorts of shenanigans. And George, he ends up working for the Yankees.

When I asked if the show was actually called *About Nothing*, Mark fell into what resembled a catatonic state of shock. Then he looked down, for a long time, at my doormat. During the period of his shock, I thought about doormats and how mine was made from a fibrous weave and, if I was remembering the back label correctly, from the furry husks of coconuts. So, did my doormat also have hair, since it shed continuously like a human head? Those poor sacrificial coconuts, cut off from their trees to make wiping mats for feet. The long silence continued. I touched my neck and felt the flush of anxiety, felt my new cultured neighbor was about to tell me that I perceived the world all wrong.

The show is called *Seinfeld*, Mark said, still counting the coconut hairs of my doormat. As in Jerry Seinfeld, and it's set in the Upper West Side.

———

I WAS SUPPOSED TO work only two weeks in November, but when an attending called out sick last minute, I volunteered to step in. Then Reese asked if I could take his Thanksgiving shift in exchange for one of my December ones. The day of turkey basting and feasting was his mother's favorite—because it was just one day, as he explained, centered around family and not like Christmas, which for the entire month of December became a part-time job.

He said he's never missed a Thanksgiving.

Not even one? I asked.

Thirty-three years and counting, he had no plans to start now.

I'd forgotten that Reese was a year younger than Madeline, though his reproductive window was much longer. Did it make sense to call it a window, if after puberty it was flung open for the rest of his life? Reese was our youngest ICU attending but by his first year had already made it onto the brochures, from his good relations with HR. For whatever reason, our HR department employed only late-middle-aged women, the same age as probably Reese's mother. He would open doors for them, wave to them in the halls, or swing by their offices for a quick chat. The HR reception counter always had a filled M&M dispenser, and I'd seen Reese stand there, chatting and pulling the handle as if it were a slot machine, *cha-ching, cha-ching*.

But a doctor who has never missed Thanksgiving was an anomaly and I asked Reese how he had managed to do that.

He shrugged. Always able to find coverage, he guessed, someone was usually willing.

I almost rescinded my offer but wanted his hours more. I wanted everybody's hours, so didn't offer him any of my shifts.

A rite of passage almost, to miss all the important holidays, to be on weekend call and never there for your family or friends. A badge of honor to have missed your sister's wedding or the major crisis of a close friend, to slowly become the person whom no one reached out to first and then the person who heard about personal news last. My brother's engagement to Tami I didn't know about until a week after it had occurred. But I texted and called you, he said, and indeed he had. He had even left a voice message that I'd meant to listen to, forgot, and while I was angry at myself for forgetting, I was also slightly proud. Because how else could you be providing great service to strangers if you didn't take that time away from people who were not?

---

ON THE SECOND FRIDAY of the month, I was summoned by the director's secretary to his corner office on the twentieth floor. The office faced northwest and had an uninterrupted view of the Hudson from bank to bank. Opposite this wall with the window was the wall of his degrees, five and counting, hung up in different types of brown frames. The latest degree was an MBA that he had finished online. The last time I was here, the degree was printed but unframed. Now it was in a frame more ornate than the one for his MD and MPH. He had a DPhil too. Prior to med school, he had studied linguistics at Oxford, a story he liked to tell new recruits during meet and greets, over drinks.

Medicine was a calling, he'd say, and sometimes you had to wait for this call while pursuing something else. Don't rush into medicine, else you'll be miserable; find new interests, challenge yourself with the unknown, etc.

Impressed by his journey, his degrees, I'd once asked the director how many languages he could speak, and he said that's not what linguistics was about. The field was about the study of languages, not any in particular. Discovering that he knew no other language, I was both disappointed and confused. Even someone like me, along with most people in the world, knew English and a second.

I worried that I was being summoned for having worked four continuous weeks. While the director cared about productivity, the hospital's HR department set limits and exceeding them was heavily discouraged. But my insane November schedule wasn't mentioned and he jumped right into praising how unflappable I'd been these last three years and essential to their program in intensive care.

He asked about my Thanksgiving plans and I said I wasn't going anywhere, since I was on service.

Good to hear, he said, and wished he could say the same. He was heading up to Westchester to see his in-laws. The wife is big on tradition, he explained. The kids like getting out of the city. That he had a wife (and kids) surprised me, and since imitation is the sincerest form of flattery, I used the same Etch A Sketch motion he used before on me when he asked if I had a father.

You have a wife? I said, swiping back and forth across my face. I didn't know about her, but it made perfect biological sense. And with her help, you became a dad. That's wonderful news.

The kids were mostly grown, in college or about to be. He listed for me their ages and I could imagine mini versions of him lining up behind him in a row. Now that it was established that we both had relatives, he asked if I wanted coffee from his Nespresso.

I said I only drank coffee from the atrium.

They do have good coffee there.

The best. It's where my father and I last spoke.

He was here?

Yes, but just to the atrium.

The director apologized again: to not have had a proper goodbye with my father, that must have been hard. I said it was to be expected. Even with the speed of international travel, sometimes you just can't get there fast enough.

Well, here's me with some good news, he announced, and started twirling a pen between his index finger and thumb like a small cheerleading baton.

For a split second, I thought he was going to say that my father was still alive, that he was downstairs waiting for me in the atrium after having spent $17.99 to park.

Can you see yourself staying at this hospital long term? he asked. And what more can I do to facilitate that?

I said I could but that my brother thinks that I am wasting my life. He's been suggesting for years that I move up to Greenwich and run a hospital there.

You certainly could, the director said slowly, but now the pen-baton was twirling faster. Any place would be fortunate to have you, but do you want to run your own hospital? To lead something like that, you would need an MBA. Meetings and politics would take over your life, mingling with hospital leadership. I suspect none of that interests you.

The director's small mouth was moving, but I was also

watching the view behind him, which was layered and hypnotic. Gray light, wintery light, but even through the fog, I could see the distant George Washington Bridge lined with cars and trucks, boats going under, a plane flying overhead.

Greenwich is too homogenous, he added. A doctor is only as good as her experience.

I agreed.

So, do you want your private office back? he asked.

I said I didn't think so.

He wiped his entire forehead thoroughly as if it were covered in sweat except it was not. He then brought up a raise and gave me an estimate of what the hospital would be willing to invest in my future.

I had him repeat the sum since it was very large. Then I asked if he really meant to give me this much and was it something like a bait and switch. Even if the raise had been a dollar, I wouldn't have been offended.

Then you are offended? he asked, clicking the pen-baton's head repeatedly.

Did you mean to offend me? I asked.

He held his right hand up in a surrender or like he was about to make a pledge. I mirrored his hand and held mine up as well.

He asked if I had a question.

I said no, not immediately.

Then why was my hand up?

Why was his?

Look, he said, putting his hand down. I don't want you to think that this only has to do with your father.

The praise resumed and I tried to keep my eyes open but it felt like being placed in the path of an oncoming train. That I was able to work through a parent's death so quickly and non-disruptively showed a great deal of character. Plain and simple, he would like to see my efforts rewarded and he personally believed that doctors like myself were the future. If he even had two more of me, he would be able to significantly reduce on other staff and improve our ranking.

Ever heard of cassette tapes? he asked.

I said I had, but his question turned out to be rhetorical and he carried on like I hadn't.

You might be too young, but cassette tapes, or tape cassettes or audio cassettes or simply cassettes, had two sides, an A and a B. They had an analog magnetic strip that you could wind and unwind, by putting your fingertip into one of the reel holes that had these tiny plastic teeth.

How he viewed my constant and comforting presence in the hospital was like that. From Joan A to B, he said, then from Joan B to A. My being a tape was music to his ears.

Why stop at cassette tape, I said, since there was no end to the number of inanimate objects I could be. What about Joan the orange? An orange being squeezed for hours to make a tall glass of refreshing juice that the hospital could drink.

He asked if he had offended me again.

No, not at all, I said. Just the opposite. I'm thrilled. And I was.

You don't sound thrilled.

But I am.

The director said he could ask for a higher raise.

I'm sorry?

He said I drove a hard bargain, which was a compliment, but he could definitely get me more money. I want the number to shock you, he said. I want to hear a good curse word out of you. Like *fuck*. An interesting fact, most English swears rely heavily on continuant-stop sound patterns. The *f* sound in *fuck*, you can hold for a very long time, but the *k* sound you can't, and this is what gives most swear words that punch. Phonaesthetics, you know what they are?

I didn't.

It's the sound-feel behind a word. How syllables are arranged to evoke an emotion or paint a picture. *Hummingbird*, for instance, has a great mouth quality to it, sounds like the bird itself flitting around and, for so many linguistic reasons, could never be a swear.

I said, Okay, sir. But honestly, I was lost. A hummingbird's wings could beat an insane number of times per second, so holding one in your mouth sounded painful.

Then his secretary of many years came in to say that we had reached the end of our time. His next meeting was waiting online, a ten-way conference call with other directors from other intensive care programs to fortify the image of a linked hospital system within our great city. But each hospital was still its own entity, and each director had a secretary. His, who was now in the room, moved in such a way that I could never catch her face. She wore black clothes and had red hair, a constant campfire ablaze on her head.

The director asked to shake my hand.

Glad we could come to an agreement, he said, my hand in his, and I left wondering where in the conversation we had disagreed.

—

LINGUISTICS OR PHONAESTHETICS WERE beyond me, but learning a language was not. My father had used cassette tapes to practice English and had pressed the player right up against his ear until the ear turned red. He would repeat the same phrases as the voice inside the machine, that by some shipment mistake, was British, and my father would try to sound like this voice, a man who called everyone chap, but end up sounding nothing like Chap, given the discordant clash of two accents.

I'd spent my earliest years speaking only to my parents, meaning I'd spent those years speaking only in Chinese. Then on my first day of kindergarten, the teacher found it so strange that while I spoke basic English, I was not entirely fluent. She called my parents in and the problem was figured out. The problem is that you are not speaking to your child in English, she announced, and my father, haltingly, said that he and my mother would continue to speak to me in whatever language they chose. But they had every faith that my English would catch up. (Because isn't learning the language why his daughter was in school, and isn't teaching the language this teacher's job?)

The teacher was skeptical, a little miffed by my father's obstinacy and implied meaning, but of course, my English would far surpass my Chinese and, like a speeding bullet, cruise through my brain.

The deeper I fell into English, the further I drifted from my parents.

*Further, farther*
*Farther, father.*
*Mother tongue* is the same in both languages.

Changing of the guards, which for most families is a gradual process but with immigrant families happens much earlier and precipitously, as the child becomes a parent.

Having English fluency in my household was like this: at any fast-food stop, I was sent in with the entire family's order and a small folded-up wad of cash. I was in charge of public ordering until Fang, once he arrived, had mastered English as well and entirely lost his accent. It was mostly the accent. Broken pronunciation implied a broken mind, unless the accent was British or French, which then meant the person was posh. For years, I was the designated telephone picker-upper and, if it was junk, the polite hanger-upper. Deepen your voice, my mother said, answer yes to your father's name or mine. If my parents had an inquiry for anyone, I was sent forth to ask. Because who could refuse a child? Or judge her for questions like Your sign for single-ply toilet paper clearly states buy one, get one free, but how come on this receipt I was still charged for two?

Come here. My father beckoning me over with the back of his hand, so I could read him a letter. A second rejection from the bank: no, they couldn't extend to him a business loan, for the same aforementioned reasons that he didn't have enough credit with them or any reputable assets like a house. What's *aforementioned*? What does that word mean?

It means "for the same reasons as in the first."

Then he and I would have to apply again. No harm in trying, he said, only in giving up.

My mother sometimes brought me along when she cleaned, so I could quickly address any concerns that a wife might have about the service. Is that eco-friendly cleaner you're using? No phthalates or ammonia? In exchange, I could sit at this family's large dining table and do homework. I could also watch the wife watch my mother. Phthalates were esters used in plastic, ammonia, the amines used in fertilizers. Already in progress was my science literacy, and the possibility that it could elevate me far and away from here.

If either Fang or I couldn't go to school—rare, but sometimes happened from seasonal flu—I was in charge of writing our sick notes for our mother to sign. But since she didn't like the sight of her own cursive, I was tasked with forging her signature as well.

I hated all of my tasks of course—the standard juvenile complaint of why me? and why did some parents clear entire forests for their children but not mine?—though with time, what I hated more was seeing my parents get bullied, for no real reason except the obvious.

Big words aside, the language of medicine has its own shorthand and lingo. Yes, the training could flatten you but it also let you into an exclusive club.

None of the jargon mattered to patients.

Give it to me simply, they and their families would request. Are you talking about the head or the heart?

I'm talking about the heart.

———

JUST THE OTHER DAY, while my mind was on my brother, mother, and the upcoming Harvest Bash, I watched a peacock cross the road. It didn't heed walk signs and all cars had to stop or go around. For a second I thought this peacock had, out of protest, escaped Connecticut and Fang's imminent petting zoo. A few blocks behind the bird was a small team of people dressed in tan custodial clothes. Had any of us seen Harry? they asked calmly, Harry being the peacock that had just run out of St. John the Divine. Everyone had seen Harry, so we all pointed frantically in the same direction to help.

When I called my brother to un-RSVP from their party, he was kind of mad-sounding, kind of livid, since they had already given their final numbers to the caterers. In both Chinese and English, the phrase is the same, "to take someone to school," "to school them in x, y, and z."

You overwork yourself, said Fang, and let yourself be bulldozed. Why are you always covering for other people but I never hear anyone covering for you? No one should be working that much. Health is wealth and time is money.

My brother could speak only in catchphrases, or only in clichés.

Had you started a private practice here, like I'd suggested, none of this would be an issue. Doctors hire other doctors under them and essentially become managers. Managing people is a skill. In time, you won't even need to practice, you just collect the fees.

With regard to leaving the hospital and starting a practice, my position has never changed. Oranges didn't abandon groves to start new ones of their own, only to manage other oranges and to never become juice. But my brother fought wars of attrition and thrived against resistance, so if only to move the lecture along, I simply told him that he was right.

In addition to Fang, I was talking more to my mother since she was calling me more to chat, and before we got started, I would confirm that she was in fact, calling me to chat.

You're a very literal person, she would say. You were not always this way. You were not a very literal child.

Here's an idea, she said, calling in the middle of the day, like yesterday and like tomorrow, to tell me something either Tami or Fang had said earlier that day.

Your brother thinks it would be better for morale if we all lived close by, within a five-mile radius.

Your sister-in-law suggested a ten-mile radius. What did you think about that?

Me? I said. What did she think about that since in either scenario, she would have to stay.

Oh, I'm not staying, she said. That's a ridiculous idea. Her ticket was booked for February and that's when she would leave. But she was just relaying these pieces of information to me. Do with them what you will.

The next time she called, they had gotten her a nanny. The they being my brother and sister-in-law, and without asking or consulting her. The nanny, a Chinese woman in her forties who reminded my mother of herself, when she was that age, doing a similar kind of work. After declaring that decade for her, the last spent in America, to be a mix of confusion and unhappiness, my mother said, What could a woman in her forties know, no offense to you or Tami. Moreover, she did not need a nanny.

Aide, I said.

All Nanny does is follow me around. I see her check the stove after I've used it. I see her tightening the knobs to make sure that I've shut off the gas. She brings me blankets before I can even ask for one. She would sit with me in the bathroom if she could. Continually boils me hot water.

It's attentive, I said.

It's a complete waste of water and electricity, she said.

I tried to change the topic. Had my mother finally seen the entire house?

She had. Every room had been viewed and sat in from every seated position, every window looked out of, and now she was bored.

They won't let me drive, my mother said, after what she deemed another incredibly boring day. They being Fang and Tami of course but also the Connecticut Department of Motor Vehicles, whom she had just finished a contentious phone call with because she had wanted to hash this situation out, once and for all, with a knowledgeable professional who would listen to her, but the professional had not. He had been as dismissive as everyone else.

They won't let you drive, Mom, because your American license expired and you never got a Chinese one. If you really want a license, we'll have to sign you up for classes and then have you retake the test.

She didn't want to retake the test, especially not one that she had already passed.

That was over thirty years ago, I said. Over thirty years ago, you passed a test.

But I still know how to drive. I still know most of the rules. In Shanghai, trains get you anywhere. Trains, buses, 24/7. You can't go anywhere here without a car. Your public transit system is a disgrace.

Is that what you told the DMV?

I didn't tell them anything that they didn't already know.

Then my mother remembered something. My mother remembered that she had a green card.

A green card is not a license, I said.

Why not?

Because a green card says nothing about your driving.

If this country is all about rights, then someone should make it so.

Boredom could breed curiosity and my phone buzzed all the time now, with questions that my mother had about us.

What does Fang do again? I know finance, but what kind?

PM stood for portfolio manager and the first time I heard the term *hedge fund,* I envisioned garden hedges and my brother pruning them with large, sharp shears. In time I learned a little more, that Fang grew other people's money, which more or less was pruning someone else's bushes into even green rows.

My mother seemed content with that explanation. Now, what do you do? I know medicine, but what kind?

I told her.

I hope you're making some money at least, she pressed on. Because in China, a doctor makes the same salary as a public school teacher. There's no difference in status or prestige between the two and work-life balance is, of course, much better for the teacher. I just hope you're not going to be destitute, Joan-na. So many doctors in America go into debt, I hear. So many say it's not worth it. And the malpractice. What are you going to do about that?

I said I'd just gotten a raise and tried, like most doctors, to avoid malpractice altogether.

I was pacing outside the seminar room where Reese was giving grand rounds. The talk was on how to demystify pulmonary hypertension, a condition with many possible causes or an unknown cause and one in which the arteries of your lungs are carrying blood at way too high of a pressure. Then dizziness, fatigue, chest pains ensue, sometimes blue-tinted skin. Pulmonary hypertension is said to develop gradually, to only worsen with time, but can possibly onset quickly and without warning, like when speaking to one's mother.

———

THE LAST TWO MONTHS of the year were packed with mandatory HR seminars that updated the staff on new behavioral regulations, like how to spot and report sexual harassment, like proper conference speaker etiquette. The latter seminar was yesterday. Studies showed that when men introduced male speakers, they stated full names and titles, but for female speakers, they used only first names, no titles. We were then instructed to introduce all speakers by their first and last names, with titles. We practiced with the person next to us. The room was half full, and mostly with women.

Today's seminar was a frequently given one on wellness. After the PowerPoint had been set up, the HR woman stood behind the computer podium and started clicking through slides titled What Is Wellness? and why it's an important quality to seek out. Wellness had been promoted to one of the behavioral competencies that all providers were required to maintain. Others included cultural competence, leadership, and nonviolent crisis intervention. I listened but kept zoning out, and when the seminar ended, I took the elevator down to the atrium café.

Only 4:45 p.m. but already pitch-black out and misty. The daytime shift was leaving, the nighttime shift entering, umbrellas opened and closed, then were sheathed in plastic.

For ten minutes, the coffee line stopped moving and I craned my neck out to see why. A cup had fallen over the counter, spraying black liquid on the floor and over a customer's shiny leather shoes. The young barista had become hands-to-mouth apologetic. Then the face on this customer, the glare, and the imminent question: You're going to remake that, aren't you? It's a very simple job. I do mine, so why can't you do yours?

From his badge, I could see that he was an MD, and from his demeanor, I already knew. Older and distinguished-looking, a believer that his special status in the hospital confers special status in the world. There were so many like him. Those who didn't bother with seminars about wellness or conference introductions, because how many conferences had they gone to already, and no complaints from any woman thus far.

The barista remade the drink. The doctor huffed off.

———

I'D NEVER SET OUT to be a gunner but once the label came up, it stuck. That I was considered the new breed of doctor made me feel like a product rolling off an assembly line to displace prior models. Medicine was getting more competitive because it was opening up to all. So by the slow force of natural selection, that doctor from the atrium café would be replaced by someone younger, better, and with knowledge more up-to-date. A question that I used to get asked was whether I was pushed into medicine, like all good Asian kids, and to this, I usually said nothing. How unscientific it was to generalize about any population and I wasn't even the most reliable source. My parents hadn't necessarily pushed me, though they also didn't stand in my way. What they did, out of pure honesty, was to remind me that there was no safety net, so whatever I chose to do, I had to do it well, I couldn't half-ass it or expect to be bailed out. Follow through, my father's advice. Stay the course.

When Reese and the director asked about my father, whenever anyone asked about my upbringing, I avoided saying too much so as to not inadvertently reveal that we'd been poor. Admitting to that had its consequences. It meant admitting to having felt less, and thus having too much to prove. A listener might think, Yes, that explains a lot, that explains a lot about you.

At every secondary school we enrolled in, Fang and I had qualified for free lunch, which our mother refused to sign us up for. No such thing as a free lunch in this country, and a Chinese saying that means the same: meat pies are never going to fall from the sky. Besides, a program like that was welfare, and being on welfare gave someone else a chance, later on, to tell you that your success was not your own.

Fang figured it out quick. The popular kids had money, or

their parents had money, which gave these kids the illusion that they did too.

Our first place in Wichita had a capacity limit of three. We were told that we would be evicted with a fourth. Not the fondest memory of my father followed, but an indelible one, the four of us sneaking into a Super 8 motel for which he had paid the price of only one guest. Once the receptionist told the other receptionist, a security guard came to block our path. We were asked to leave even before my father started flipping them off. For a small fee, an older Chinese couple with no kids took us in for a month, before my father decided we were moving to Scranton. The room was in the back of their one-story ranch, hidden from view by a tall evergreen bush they planted by no coincidence after we arrived. We were forbidden from walking where we could be seen or using the kitchen during the day.

I was never hungry, never without clothes or proper shelter, but the second the woman saw me go in the bathroom, she started pounding on the door. It was either that or the projects, and we were not going to live in the projects.

A good memory. A fond one. The most frugal member of our family and yet my father would end up doing the most unfrugal of things. Spend a week's worth of dishwashing money, for instance, on what he promised to be a surprise. We wondered what it could be. Maybe bed frames, since we had been sleeping on floor mattresses all this time. Weeks passed and we forgot about it. Then on our last day of school, the first of summer, he and my mother picked us up in a lime-green Mustang, rented for the afternoon. There was nothing more American to him than American cars, American muscle, because inside a car like that, even the weak could feel strong. We blasted the radio and went to the nearest Wendy's drive-through. My father pulled the car beyond the intercom and I stuck my head out of the rear window to place the order. Everything on the value menu and two cups of hot water. Yes, just hot water. My father drove us to a park and we ate in the car. Then he drove around an empty parking lot as fast as he could, while my mother kept hitting him in the arm and telling him to slow down. Bystanders must have said, Whatever the story is there, those people are reckless and certainly living beyond their means. They then told their kids, Kids, this is why the poor stay poor and the rich stay rich.

Probably that day was one of the times my mother reminded me that a woman needed power, and power came from money, so a woman needed money.

I wouldn't admit to being poor in conversation, but for colleges, on paper, I did. Below a certain household income, some of the best schools were free. Then you applied for book allowances each semester and winter coat funds. You ate only at dining halls, never out. Fang got a full ride first and helped me do the same. Forms like these were straightforward enough to fill out. We had been filing our parents' taxes for years.

Merit-based scholarships, we told our parents, who we both agreed never needed to know. But had my mother just checked, she would have seen that neither place Fang or I went to offered merit-based aid.

Certain Americans could be two-faced. Acquaintances and other parents from our school made their implications about us clear.

You must be so proud of your children.

But how had your son really gotten into Yale? Because Yale looks out for minorities. They save a certain percentage of seats for them.

How had your daughter really gotten into Harvard? Because Harvard is even easier on minorities and on women too.

Settling the question that I'd always had then. No success of mine had anything to do with me, my work ethic, or my brain.

During college, Fang began coming back home in newer and more expensive clothes.

Scholarship money? my mother would ask, rubbing the lapel of his blue wool blazer with gold buttons, but perhaps already knowing full well that it wasn't. Borrowed from a roommate. But in short order he was able to afford his own.

Fang in his late twenties, taking me out to lunch. I was a senior at Harvard then, and he had driven up from Manhattan, where he'd just been promoted to associate of something, or in my own head, the associate of money. No more D-hall food for once, and I could pick any place I liked. I requested Asian food, some semblance of what our mother would've made, which the D-hall never served. Think bigger, he told me, arriving outside my dorm, dressed in fine long linen pants and a cashmere T-shirt sweater, before I knew that T-shirt sweaters were a thing. Per his suggestion, we went to a French restaurant, Boston's most expensive, where in the parking lane, I watched him toss his new Audi car keys to a white valet and say, Take care of this for me, will you? and then tip this man fifty bucks.

Inside, I had my own white server who stood next to me the entire time like a bodyguard. Each crumb that fell out of my mouth, he scooped away with a silver scraper. Warm bread slices were held out to me with silver tongs. And then when I had to use the restroom, my bodyguard followed, opened the soundproof bathroom door, closed the soundproof door, and stood outside while I peed.

Did I remember anything about the food? The actual taste of it? No. I wanted my mother's food the entire time.

Back at the table with our bodyguards, my brother asked whom I had befriended at Harvard, whom I'd connected with. Because I was, he said, at the most well-connected place in the country, the starting place of future presidents, industry scions, CEOs, CFOs, COOs, and Silicon Valley tycoons.

I hated this. Hated the sense that I got from Fang that there was some magical beanstalk I had to climb. Nothing good comes from climbing beanstalks, didn't he know that? There are giants up there.

But Fang did know. The whole point was to climb to the giants and become a giant yourself.

Jiu-an, don't think you're any less, he said, and then sipped his Scotch at half past noon.

This is our chance, don't throw it away.

What is learned outside of the classroom is just as important as what you learn in it, if not more.

Meet the right people. They can open the right doors.

Wouldn't it be cool if someday you became a senator's wife?

(The famed MRS degree, because in practice, a female brain is worth nothing. Four lobes of the cerebrum, and I have sometimes imagined one of mine labeled RAGE.)

After my brother said those things, I realized that he and I had officially diverged. Siblings grew apart gradually, but, on that day, it felt like a cliff and then a crash. I let him talk to me that way because, as a young adult, I had started to recognize guilt, that I'd had our parents since birth and he had not. This point he never brought up, but I could sense between us, he had been left behind. Spoiled, Fang must have thought of me, to have had both Mother and Father all to myself, when he needed them the most. Our mother didn't hold his hand for long enough, and by the time he saw her again, he was too old.

But as I watched Fang instruct his bodyguard to bring us an assortment of desserts, I felt he had still let me down. Just as I didn't know about having an older brother until he appeared, I suddenly knew that I once had a brother, but now he was gone.

———

THREE PIECES OF MAIL:

A Shen Yun brochure—5,000 years of civilization reborn.

A silken envelope, in an off-white color in between alabaster and champagne. I untied the satin ribbon that was around it and saw that I was cordially invited to Fang and Tami's annual Winter Bash, the pinnacle of their bashes since there were so many December holidays to celebrate. I didn't bother reading through the activities, the list of which was long and embossed in gold foil lettering. I was definitely not going to go but debated how to get that message across. If I never RSVP'd, my brother would RSVP for me. If I called to un-RSVP again, I would get another lecture. Texting was the safest but say Fang texted back immediately with a reprimand and an urgency to talk. What's more important than family? And I know you're getting my texts, Jiu-an. I know because from my end, I can see when my texts are being marked as read, a setting I've told you to turn off for your own benefit but you keep forgetting to do.

The third piece of mail was the strangest. From an unaddressed and vaguely named Asian cultural center, a twenty-nine-page leaflet, all in Chinese, that on the cover wished me peace with a drawing of a female celestial being. The first few pages were about health and how to find your inner serenity. But then the rest of the pages discussed the most effective ways to withdraw from the Chinese Communist Party, and once I realized what I was reading, I carefully set the booklet down and pushed it away.

———

I WAS ASSIGNED TO just one service week in December, and looking at my almost blank schedule in my hospital account, wiping my monitor down to see the twenty-four blank boxes more clearly, I decided that that wouldn't do. I couldn't be given a raise for no work. It felt like negligence, theft, like I was only taking from the system and not giving back. I let the other attendings know that I was more than available to step in at any time, no strings attached, and soon I was on service the entire month again, with two Sundays off.

The first Sunday I dedicated myself to cleaning my apartment. I owned a robot vacuum that swept around with no foreseeable plan, taking a different path each time, often driving itself into a corner. Then it beeped to tell me that it was stuck. Like the man in my father's cassette player, a female voice lived in my vacuum. But she was American, and when she came on to say *error,* I heard *terror,* like the woman was afraid.

To Fang, a circular vacuum for square rooms made no sense, and he suggested that I hire a cleaner.

I said our mother used to do that, clean other people's houses and wipe away their filth.

That's the past, said Fang. The past is the past. The future is now.

Tami had asked if the robot vacuum was my surrogate child. You like to worry about the vacuum, she said, and that worry becomes an activity in and of itself that fills you up.

Once I passed thirty, many things had, according to some, become my surrogate child. If I bent down to admire a dog around Tami, it became my child. If I stared too long at a clock, it became my biological clock. Once I passed thirty-five, the frequency of child references doubled.

As I was cleaning Robot Vacuum, cutting from around its bristles a lawn of black hair that should've left me bald, my mother called to say that there was no one in the house except Nanny and her.

Why's that? I asked, trying to pry hair that once belonged to me out of my first surrogate child. But I was unsuccessful and decided to put Robot Vacuum in the closet for a time-out.

Terror, it cried, and my mother asked what that was and I said I didn't hear anything, while shutting the closet door.

She said everyone else left to do holiday shopping.

I didn't like shopping either, I said, to which she replied who said she didn't like it? All women liked to shop, and had she the stamina to keep up with Tami for a day, she would've gone.

My sister-in-law was a committed shopper and knower of

name brands. Her only policy for herself was to never buy any-thing on sale or visit outlet malls where crowds of Asian women gathered, looking for deals. If you couldn't afford luxury prod-ucts at full price, Tami believed, you shouldn't be buying them at all. But sometimes I wondered if in steering herself away from one stereotype, she'd steered herself straight into another.

My mother added that not only did all women like to shop, but they liked to shop together.

I couldn't say that I agreed.

Well, have you ever tried? Have you asked Tami to take you with her?

The only time I'd gone with her into a store, we were quickly and immediately ushered into a private room. When I asked what kind of place was this, both Tami and the sales-clerk blinked at me: You've never been inside a Tiffany's? Who's Tiffany? I'd asked, and neither of them seemed to know or care. We were in that private room for the better half of a day, admiring shiny pieces on velvet trays, while mannequin-like men in black suits kept bringing us champagne.

And you didn't like that? my mother asked. Drinking free champagne at a jewelry store?

I said I didn't like jewelry. The champagne was all right.

My mother said nothing. There was just silence on the other end. We moved on and spoke about something else.

But I could tell that she was disturbed or at least put off, and after we counted to three and hung up, I went outside for a quick walk. I strolled along Morningside Drive and to the hos-pital, where out in front were two calm nurses smoking on a bench next to an ambulance that had driven up the curb.

A man, biologically, has one X chromosome and one Y. A

woman has two X. The X chromosome is much bigger than the Y, has more genes on it, more variations, etc. A woman is XX, a genetic fact that has always read to me like math. Let X be a random variable, an unknown. What's X? I'd never felt particularly womanly nor did I seem to know what being one entailed. Did it require liking certain things? Shopping, jewelry, children. And if none of that interested you, was it like three strikes and you're out? The Yankees had no women.

At the end of my walk, I remembered that I liked flowers. No sunflowers or roses, but dried flowers, wildflowers, ferns, and succulents. Hydrangeas especially, their petals, with the blue color seeming to lift off them as if evaporating into thin air. Chocolate of all kinds, from bittersweet baking blocks to chocolate-covered strawberries. But did liking both flowers and chocolate make the woman a woman, or did that make her a girl?

———

COMING BACK FROM HIS own meeting with the director, Reese was in a bad mood. He went straight to the back of the office, to the refreshments station, where there was now a bin of foam stress balls thanks to another HR woman, but not the same ones who gave the seminars. Reese picked up three balls and started to juggle them in front of me.

My universal advice to patients is best to never know your doctors personally. Best never to hear them emote or confess their love for someone. At this point, I could never in good faith allow Reese to provide me care. I would never be able to sign the waiver.

From balls, he said while juggling, you can graduate to rings or clubs. In quick succession, he threw the three foam balls at me, none of which I caught as I was unprepared and he had aimed them mostly overhead.

You have to reach, Joan. You have to reach your arm out and catch, like so. He demonstrated, then he flexed. Now throw them back. Come on. Throw them back like I threw them to you.

Months ago, before my father died, Reese, out of the blue, asked Madeline and me if we thought he would make a good dad. She and I looked at each other to decide how we were going to handle this, and before we could respond, he said he thought he would. Which was why he wanted to become one, because he knew that he would do a good job of it once given the chance. Two tasks that he considered exceptionally fatherly were teaching the child how to ride a bike and teaching the child how to throw. Things his father had taught him that he was now ready to pass on. A nice moment in the office in which I knew Reese was being vulnerable and I didn't want to ruin it by saying that my father taught me neither and that you could probably be a good enough dad without having to. Kids don't really know any better and can be happy with very little.

Because Reese wasn't my father, I declined throwing the stress balls back to him and placed them in a row on my desk.

He finally calmed down and sat, lacing his hands behind his head. He asked if I thought he made a good doctor, and it was a question that I didn't want to answer anymore since I'd already answered it last year and the year before. The same answer being that he was neither the best nor the worst, which is where all of us were. Moving into a shared office has taught me that some people required more encouragement, water, and sun. Some people were just like plants.

Instead, I said Why, had the director reprimanded him?

No, not quite. But he hadn't said anything positive.

No news is good news, I reminded him, and that excess praise could stunt a person.

For once, Reese was quiet and staring up at the ceiling, straight into the fluorescent lights. These lights were strong, and I feared that if he stared long enough, he would burn through his retina and blind himself like one of those tragic heroes, like Icarus.

Hey, Reese? Reese, look over here please.

Fun fact, he said, not looking over and continuing to blanch his eyeballs. I'm still a hundred thou in debt, accruing sixty dollars of interest a day. What I really need is a raise, and I'm happy about yours—the director brought it up, actually, kept mentioning your schedule this month and last as exemplary— but it's not like I haven't been working. I've worked all of my shifts, except for the one that we traded, that you didn't want me to pay you back for. Outside of national holidays, when do I ever shirk duties? I don't do nights because I need my sleep, and I'm far too senior to be working shifts reserved for new-comers or people who function well at night. After I explained all this to the director, he still didn't seem too convinced. I said he could force me to work nights, but it truly wouldn't be in the best interest of the patients. I'm not Joan, I said, nor do I try to be. I'm my own person and at peace with what works best for me. But should that mean that I go unrecognized? Does that mean I should keep getting passed over?

—

SMELLS OF CINNAMON, NUTMEG, and vanilla permeated the ninth floor, and a one-foot-diameter wreath had been placed on 9B's door and mine. Did I do that? I asked myself when I first saw the green ring with red bows and berries, because sometimes I forgot these things, what I did or didn't do outside of the hospital, like the real world had become a dream. No, the wreath finding and putting had to have been Mark.

Through the double set of windows, Enormous Man was visible one day and gone the next. A two-foot-tall evergreen wrapped in tinsel had been put up on the sill, and this new potted plant blocked a third of the view.

I heard tenants outside all the time now. The door of apartment 9B opened and closed, echoey corridor talk between my neighbor and someone else. Without even looking out the peephole, I knew that people were entering and exiting 9B with books or tools or pies.

The doorman continued to ask whether or not I was in love with Mr. Mark. Had I been showered with gifts yet? he asked, for that was crucial to finding love. A constant stream of them. Women like stuff.

When I said I had less stuff than Mark, the doorman didn't seem to believe me, but then as if on cue, as if he and Mark had conspired together, been discussing me behind my back, Mark found me later that day to ask if I needed a reading chair. He'd bought a new leather one for himself, but his previous non-leather one was still in fine shape, and before he put it up for sale, he thought that he would check.

Had the doorman put him up to this?

Who?

The doorman. Our doorman. The one obsessed with rom-coms and matchmaking, who won't push the elevator buttons for you or let you push them yourself unless you're standing dead center in the suspended metal box with good posture.

Mark knew nothing about this; no one escorted him to the elevators or commented on his posture.

Maybe he likes you, said Mark.

He's married, I said.

Mark's eyes did a big and exaggerated spin. No, not like that. He likes you as a tenant. A very New York thing to have happened. Most doormen have favorites, ones they try to look out for and help.

How to become un-favorited was my thought.

It's a good thing, he said, and went back to his apartment to bring out the chair.

The moment I saw it, I loved it. A vibrant, showstopping chartreuse suede, in a slightly retro design. With a swipe of my hand, the suede turned from a light to a darker chartreuse; another swipe and it turned from dark back to light. I offered to pay, but Mark waved off even the thought. He pushed the chair into 9A and my open living room, which just had an old futon I'd bought years ago and in one corner my robot vacuum, in another the books that he had given me that had gone unread. I moved the old futon to the back and put Suede Chair in the room's center.

Did you get robbed? he asked, looking around, and I said not that I knew of.

But where's your table, where do you eat?

I had a fold-out chair and table in the closet, a desk in the bedroom where sometimes I ate. From the closet, I brought out the metal chair and unfolded it.

Please, I said.

He said it was the most uncomfortable thing he'd ever sat in.

But then there we were, me in Suede Chair, receiving my first guest since I'd moved in. Given the neighborhood's safety index and that my one bed was too small, Fang and Tami never visited. I also wasn't close to any famous museums, for educational purposes, for their boys.

I told Mark I didn't know how guest visits were supposed to go. Did he ask me questions or did I? He laughed. I laughed. Then he added that for all his time in the city, he had never met anyone like me.

You haven't met enough people, I replied. There were lots of people like me, tucked away in schools and office buildings. People who had been standardized, a standard provider who provides standardized care.

No, you're different, he said.

A word I hated hearing about myself and must have given that away through my immediate frown.

Different is good, he said, shifting in his chair that was actually too small for him and creaking a lot from new weight. Some people try their whole lives to be different and never achieve it in any significant way. Some people make it look effortless.

I frowned some more though Mark didn't seem to notice and continued to inspect my empty room aloud. His words started to echo so I stopped paying attention to them.

Who really wanted to be different? I wondered. And to be

treated differently for things about them that couldn't be changed. Most people who were different just wanted to be the same.

———

THE FIRST COUNSELOR DEDUCED that I had trouble seeing boundaries. My arm-crossing father, who came to initial meetings, replied that boundaries were a Western trait, a luxury, an act of selfishness. No such boundary existed within our family as the self does not exist, and if the self does not exist, then there can be nothing to invade. My father also added that I seemed fine and these meetings were stupid.

We can see how you would think so, the counselor said, but we worry about your daughter. An excellent student but has trouble connecting with peers, is rigid, inflexible, things have to be done a certain way according to Joan, according to her peers. She should be tested for . . . , and each counselor gave a list.

She's shy, said my father.

But sometimes she has outbursts.

Is she physically violent?

No one is suggesting that.

Then I don't see a problem.

We're not suggesting there is a problem. We too want Joan to succeed.

Does she need your permission to do that? he wanted to ask, but couldn't get it out clearly and the counselor didn't seem to understand him. She needs no one's permission, not mine, not yours, and because this was the extent of his English while angry and arm-crossed, he just repeated the phrase—not mine, not yours—until it was time for us to go.

The last counselor I saw was in college, freshman year. She asked if I had ever met with a counselor who was more like myself. A well-meaning question that she asked cautiously and in a circular way, at 7:30 a.m., before I had class at 8:00. I think the word she didn't want to use was *Asian*. The nonexistent Asian therapist—had I ever met one of those? To understand difference requires difference and someone who has been in your shoes. At least she was the first counselor to admit not quite getting it instead of trying to pinpoint a fault. After her I would have no more time for counselors, and once I started my training, I needed only to turn to the person beside me in lecture to know that we were the same. At face value, medicine was still a meritocracy and the most straightforward path that I could take. Moving through the ranks had less to do with what I looked like or my family, but had everything to do with if I could watch and listen carefully, if I could carry out the tasks that were asked of me and then pass the same instructions on when my turn came to teach. The joy of having been standardized was that you didn't need to think beyond a certain area. Like a death handled well, a box had been put around you, and within it you could feel safe.

——

HAD MY FATHER BEEN happy raising me, been happy to be my father? And had I posed those questions to him, would he have considered them important questions or simply Western ones?

Americans he found to be so outwardly happy all the time and superficially positive. To be indiscriminately happy seemed to him as much of a curse as to be indiscriminately sad.

We often went months without speaking, not out of annoyance with each other or any real reason except that there wasn't a need. The longest stretch was a year in my mid-twenties when I was body-deep in clerkships and my father was, as usual, busy. I spoke to my mother that year and to him indirectly through her. Tell Dad about this, and she said that she would. The year of no contact ended just as casually as it began. He called me about his vertigo, a possible ear infection, and some red fungal spots on his chest. I asked if he had seen a doctor, and he said wasn't I the doctor, his daughter the doctor, unless the doctor was not in today and it was just his daughter. If just the latter was in, he would call back tomorrow for the doctor.

My father could be playful, mixed in with Asian stoicism and formality. I said no, the doctor was here today and ready to receive patients.

Then we went through his symptoms and I told him the kind of medication to buy and how often to put it on.

It was a twenty-minute conversation, one of the longest that we would have.

Thanks, doctor-daughter. Or do you prefer daughter-doctor? Which one?

I said the former was fine.

All right then, doctor-daughter, so long, goodbye.

But the phrase for goodbye in Chinese is *zài jiàn,* or "see you again."

———

TO WRITE A CHINESE word, we sometimes do it in halves. On the left-hand side, we can put a person (人) on top of an ocean wave (巳) and, on the right-hand side, give this wave-riding person a knife (刀). A knife for fighting with, for striving with; a knife to accompany you on the unknown sea adventure ahead.

*Chuàng* (创): to create something that never was, to forge a new path, to innovate, to achieve, to strive; anything worth doing requires a person to *chuàng*.

I did have Mark to thank for my new book stack that rose a foot and a half beside Suede Chair like a stalagmite. I'd gone through each book again, reading titles and back cover summaries, maybe even the first page. One in particular, the smallest and thinnest book, caused my heart to skip and accelerate, then, I thought, to stop altogether. *The Old Man and the Sea,* but another title could have been *Father*. I read it, on and off, over the next few days and found in it everything that Mark had talked about. Baseball and homage to a player whom the old man believes to be the greatest of all time—"have faith in the Yankees, my son. Think of the great DiMaggio." The old man is a fisherman and has suffered eighty-four days of no fish. On the eighty-fifth day, he catches a marlin and, in his quest to bring the big fish home and sell it at market, he is attacked by sharks that have caught the scent of the marlin's blood. The old man fights the sharks, punching some in the nose, killing several with his spear. More sharks appear and eventually devour the marlin, leaving only its skeleton. The old man, however, survives, makes it ashore, and stumbles home.

I liked this line, and even found a pencil to give the sentence a light underline: "He rested sitting on the un-stepped mast and sail and tried not to think but only to endure."

On December 10, an inch of snow fell. Because of this inch, families flocked to Central Park with makeshift sleds (kitchen trays and laundry baskets). To slide down, each kid had to be dragged up first, and by the end of the day the initially white hill was left scratched and brown. I felt bad for this hill. Nature was supposed to dominate the child, not the reverse.

Snow in the city was usually light. Snow in Michigan meant snow that came down continuously. Each time I would look out a new foot had appeared until the window was half covered and the door was frozen shut. The two winters we spent in Bay City, my father took Fang and me to a ski mountain each January and bought us both day passes. For the next eight hours, he promised to be in the lodge, but for the sake of getting the most value out of our tickets, he asked us not to come find him unless it was an emergency, unless we were concussed.

*Chuàng,* he would bellow, and make his hand into a fist.

Without instruction, I started going downhill. I went down straight, not knowing how to turn, thus only accelerating. Each time I fell, the board flew over my head and I somersaulted from momentum. One, two, three, and laughing from the thrill of three somersaults, I would smash my teeth into the snow that had hardened into ice.

*Chuàng* is supposed to feel like that—a mix of danger and joy, pleasure and pain.

———

THE SECOND SUNDAY I had off, I trained to Greenwich again to see my mother. Fang was away on a work trip, and Tami and the boys were at a holiday auction for school. I knocked for only five minutes before a new staff member opened the door, the aide, five two, 127 pounds. She knew how I liked to visit from the housekeeper and, without a word beyond that, led me through the foyer, down the hall.

My mother and I sat, once more, in the kitchen. The aide boiled water and made hot chocolate from it. She put the mugs in front of us and shook up a can of whipped cream. If you asked my mother, she would never admit to having a sweet tooth. But how my mother took her whipped cream: Tell me when to stop, and she would never say stop, she would have you keep your finger on the nozzle until you physically could not. The aide already seemed to know this and filled another much larger cup entirely with cream before passing it to my mother along with a tiny gold spoon.

As she took her sip of hot chocolate and then ate a spoonful of whipped cream, I stared amazedly at her, at some of the weight she had gained back in her cheeks, probably from the pure butterfat. Before leaving the room, the aide drew the curtains to let in more light.

You look younger, I said.

I'm older, my mother said, and blew on the steam. They tell me that you aren't coming to their Winter Bash. The last two words she said in English, but instead of *bash,* she said *rash*. They tell me you aren't coming to their winter rash.

Fang and I had texted about it, I replied, and he'd already scolded me on everyone else's behalf, so.

She said the issues between him and me she could guess at. She was our mother, after all. Children don't change that much, she declared, they have their personalities as babies, as toddlers, and then they keep those same personalities as adults. But why did Tami and I not get along?

I said we got along fine.

But you're not friends.

No.

She's not a big sister to you.

And I wasn't a little sister to her.

You know what they say about Chongqing women, about women from Chongqing like Tami?

That they're beautiful? Because that's what my mother said about women in every Chinese city. No part of China had ugly women, it seemed, except Beijing, where the studious, short-haired women lived and ate crispy duck.

Don't be insubordinate, she told me. Don't interrupt me while I'm elucidating. I was going to say that yes, while the women there are very stunning, they also know how to live a good life. But a person should also know how to live a hard one, so she can appreciate the good.

I asked what my mother was really trying to say.

It's a shame Tami doesn't work anymore, isn't it?

I said you couldn't say those things about women, especially not in suburban America.

But was Tami an ordinary suburban woman? my mother asked. She had come here all on her own, she had entered this country on her own merit, on a student visa for graduate school. Why study so hard to achieve all that, just to marry and be a mom?

Three kids are a lot.

It's not four or twenty.

But it's not zero.

A woman needs something else that is hers alone. Children leave. Children are not always yours.

Am I not yours? I asked slowly, staring down into my hot chocolate.

That's a complicated question.

It's a yes or no question.

You believe that, she said and then nothing. She tried to blow on her steam, but the hot chocolate had cooled.

———

THE SAME CABDRIVER CAME to pick me up and pulled over after the same red light. He asked after my mother, and I said her physical health was much improved.

Twenty minutes spent in thought and feeling the wind of passing cars rock the cab from side to side.

My brother's type has always been Chinese, and not American born but mainland. The more money he made, the sleeker his girlfriends became. With Tami, I saw that he had perfected his type. The first time we met, they were both working in finance and living together on the southernmost tip of Manhattan, in Battery Park City. The apartment had a dead-on view of a green blip that turned out to be the Statue of Liberty. I had to move to New York, my brother insisted, since at the time I was still studying in Boston. Once I moved here, the three of us could be close and have meals together, and perhaps his hope was that his future wife and I would be friends.

Tami was the only child of high school teachers who had pushed her academically until she rose to the top of her class in every class and was sent to Beijing for college, where she continued to excel. Then from Beijing to New York for a master's in data science and where, at a hibachi grill, she connected with Fang through mutual friends.

She liked to remind me that she was older, but she was not that much older, three years.

That half day spent at Tiffany's, Tami was there to buy their wedding bands and to have her engagement ring cleaned. Both of us seemed to realize that we weren't going to be friends but perhaps we could still be friendly.

She declared that she wanted to buy me something, anything that I liked. The saleswoman cooed after me. Lucky girl. More commission.

I said I didn't need anything.

You won't let me buy you a gift, snapped Tami. What do you have against Tiffany's? The implication being what did I have against her.

Wearing something from here makes you legitimate. Status, she said, her silver bracelet jangling on her wrist like a price tag. Don't be ungrateful, Joannie. When I was your age, I would have jumped at the chance to shop here.

When she was my age, three years ago, at twenty-four, she hadn't yet met my brother. A short courtship began after their hibachi meal but since the work visa keeping her here was set to expire, a decision was made to speed up the process. I didn't want to think this but I did. The most American of mentalities crept in. Beautiful and smart Chinese girl from Chongqing meets my brother, steals my brother, and uses him as a means to an end. Overlooking the fact that she was working many hours in finance as well and would for another two years, until she became pregnant with their first child. Overlooking also the fact that she and my brother had similar core values and were very much in love.

Height and physique—wise they were well matched. At five nine, my sister-in-law reminded me of an integral sign or the elegant f-holes of a violin. Fang somehow got the height gene and grew five inches past our father to six one. Then thanks to trainers and a high-protein diet, he bulked up to become the shape of his namesake, a square.

When I finally moved to New York for residency, they had already settled down in Greenwich with their first son, a second on the way. Greenwich, they said, that's where you're supposed to move next. To start your private practice, to buy your first home. The boys needed cousins. An aunt and uncle who lived close by. Fang believed that a family should grow in the most normal way possible. Weird was for later. Three or four generations down the line we could afford to be weird.

I lost my brother the day he decided to become my parent.

Obvious, of course. Immigrant father achieves very little and immigrant son, seeking to outdo the father, achieves the level of mind-boggling success that could only happen in America. Soon, Mind-boggling Rich Son starts a family of his own and becomes the new patriarch on this continent and assumes he knows best.

Interrupting my thoughts was the kind cabdriver, who had turned the heater up for me. How we doing back there? he said, shouted over the noise of the fan. Toasty? No rush.

—

TWICE IN DECEMBER, I heard, then spotted, in my neighborhood a caravan of festive RTVs rolling south down Broadway, then east along 110th. The RTVs were decorated in red and green gift wrap, their drivers were dressed in green onesies, with elf hats, and for a mile radius anyone could hear the song being blasted, Santa Claus was coming to town. Cars and buses made way; pedestrians stopped crossing the street. Then at the very end of the parade Santa Claus did come on the back of a red monster truck with monster wheels, dancing, hip shaking, in traditional red getup, with reflective aviator sunglasses and a full black beard. I was stunned each time I saw this but, like all the parents and children on the sidewalk, waved to Santa both times.

—

TATER TOTS DAY IN the hospital cafeteria, and I had just scooped a full plate and gone out to find a seat. Reese was at a table eating a sad deli sandwich alone, no tater tots. When I went to sit down next to him, pushing the tray of fried goodness into the table middle for both of us to share, he didn't greet me like usual but started talking as if I'd been sitting there all along.

Yesterday, he had an epiphany, he said.

About? I asked.

About recognizing some hard truths with respect to his situation. The first being that he didn't belong at this hospital anymore, or any hospital; the second, more severe—he asked if I was ready for it and I said I would brace myself—the second being that he's never belonged in medicine to begin with. In hindsight, what was he really doing with his life? All these years trying to fit himself into a mold when maybe he was never meant to fit a mold, but the reverse.

I asked what was the reverse.

That the mold was meant to fit him. That he was the mold.

You're the mold, I said. Which, when said aloud, didn't sound quite right and only reminded me of fungi.

I asked if this had anything to do with my raise.

No way, he said. Haven't thought about that in ages. The deli meat in his sandwich drooped, the lettuce was already soggy.

I said he would get his own raise soon; I could see it coming around the corner.

But from here on out, they'll give them all to you, he replied. That's how it works. Once they identify someone, that person reaps all the rewards. When it comes down to it, Joan, you truly belong in this profession, whereas I'm not so sure I ever did. Compared with you, I'll never be good enough. A terrible feeling, being average or below. I'm sure you've never experienced it, so you have no idea what I'm going through, but it's a gutted feeling right here.

He put a hand on his chest. I lost my appetite for tots.

What else would you do? I asked.

He said he had asked himself the same question, which precipitated another more horrifying epiphany about his lack of a legacy, should he continue down his current path of mediocrity. A man needs a career legacy, he emphasized, whereas a woman doesn't always have to worry about that, a woman doesn't have the same pressures.

I said I cared about career legacy; I had the same pressures as he did in that realm and wanted to be more than just somebody's wife.

He seemed caught off guard to hear me say that. He explained he was using "woman" in the abstract, he didn't mean me specifically.

Oh, I said, and he continued to talk about this abstract woman as if I had no skin in the game.

A woman biologically is able to reproduce, he said, and should she choose to, her legacy would be secure, without concerns for what else she can offer the world since she has already given it a human being. But a man can't get pregnant on his own. A man must forge his own legacies and create something out of nothing.

I tried to act surprised by his statements, to lift my eyebrows a little and show that I hadn't realized this before, that Reese, being a male, didn't have ovaries that released one egg each month to be fertilized, and if this egg isn't fertilized by one sperm out of an onslaught, the sixteen-millimeter-thick uterine lining that had readied itself to support the fertilized egg, the zygote, would shred, each month, bit by bit, and come out the uterus like a vine of ripe tomatoes put through the blender.

I said while I didn't know this abstract woman personally, I imagined that once she met her abstract man, she would probably tell him to fuck right off.

Fuck right off? he asked.

Yeah, like that.

Perplexed but not necessarily offended, he said it seemed too early in the day for swear words and he didn't quite know what I meant.

—

DEATHS SOAR THE LAST week of December, and New Year's Day is consistently the deadliest day of the year. Weather, influenza, car accidents, substance abuse around the holidays, stress of family, of eating, and of constantly having to be jolly, but no verifiable cause has been found.

It was a resident's first Christmas working and a few hours in, she had reached her most sad. Every batch of them went through cycles of sadness, and should you come across one at peak sadness, they would pull you aside to emote that no one told them what it was like. Being a doctor, that is. Kind of dull actually, much more busy work than expected, checking numbers then rechecking them, grueling but dull, the same routine each day.

Nurses, on the other hand, very rarely fell into a slump or seemed to have existential crises. They didn't carry themselves with gravitas, and if they needed a break from the drama, they simply took five minutes outside, then came back recharged. Nurses brought in pans of homemade lasagna and plates of sugar cookies to be shared. They decorated the residents' lounge with snowmen wearing telemetry boxes, each snowman bearing a resident's name. The nurses in our unit comforted the resident for missing her first Christmas by congratulating her on the first badge of honor, and here, have a cookie, two scoops of lasagna, fresh out of the microwave.

You don't have to care about people to be a doctor, but you do to be a nurse.

You don't need a sense of humor as a doctor, but it helps as a nurse.

The days between Christmas and New Year are called the "perineum," an older nurse told a younger one at the bay. You know what that means, don't you?

From anatomy. The perineum: in males the pyramidal surface region between anus and scrotum; in females, between anus and vulva.

———

DURING THE WEEK OF perineum, I found at my apartment door a Samsung television on a stand. I knocked on Mark's door and told him through the wood that his stuff was again blocking my path and preventing me from going inside.

My TV? he said, coming out. Your TV. Surprise. The best holiday gifts are those we least expect! Or don't think to ask for.

The Samsung had served him well until he recently bought himself a new one. Nothing was wrong with the old set, and he didn't want to be one of those people who threw out electronics every year. It seemed wasteful to him when people upgraded phones whenever possible and he himself had an iPhone model so old it wasn't even available anymore, the software inside no longer supported. He showed me his phone, which had a long crack down the screen and was very small. He looked incredibly proud, and I thought of my cousin who, when showing me her big-screen phone encased in plastic rhinestones and gold, looked equally proud. My father believed quite strongly that East and West would never get along, never see eye to eye. But maybe they could, I now thought, since Mark and my cousin would never fight over the same phone.

Long story short, he said, please take it.

The phone? I asked.

No, the TV. A TV could also help me unwind, and after that last visit, and sitting in that horrible little chair, he found my apartment too vacant. Had he not known I lived there, he would've assumed no one did. Then he started talking about voids and how no one should have to live in them or ever see that word in print. Void should be avoided, he said and because I was too tired to say otherwise, we moved my new-old television set inside during this speech. He told me to call the cable company tomorrow, he texted me a number. If I wasn't home during any of their slots, he offered to oversee the installation process for me, for a small fee.

Sure, I said and he looked wide-eyed back at me and said that he was kidding. Why would there be a fee? We've been decent neighbors to each other, he'd hoped, possibly even friends?

I nodded and he smiled, running a hand through his hair, voluminous today, with height at the front.

I smiled too but nervously since Mark needed to leave so I could shower, eat, and prep for another shift tomorrow. Grime and sweat were rolling down my back, and under my coat, my scrubs were splattered with blood. I would have taken off my coat already but didn't want the red streaks to freak my neighbor out and cause him to faint.

With the television and stand pushed up against my west-facing wall, Mark worried that the glare from the windows could shoot in and compromise my visibility. We should move the television to the other wall, he said, turn the Suede Chair around and try that. But then he noticed that my coaxial outlet was on the west-facing wall, so if we turned the entire setup around, cable lines would have to be discreetly run along the baseboards.

Right, I said.

But really, which wall do you prefer? He would have to tell the cable guy when he came.

Had I agreed to let Mark oversee the installation? I must have, but somehow, I couldn't remember when and how that had gone. I said both walls seemed reasonable.

Neither of us moved or said anything after that. The room was dim, and Mark stood in the shadows, staring at the baseboard, as if waiting for something to appear. Then, instinctively, I knew. I went to my kitchen drawer and pulled from it the spare key to apartment 9A. I jingled it by the key ring like a tea bell. Was this it? The silver of the key was reflective and shiny, and once Mark saw what I was holding, his expression changed.

Pocketing the key, he said it would be an honor, and heading out the door, he expressed gratitude and enthusiasm that we had become, as he had hoped, true neighbors in the New York City sense of the word.

—

I CALLED.

We're having a limited time offer on two hundred channels, said a deep, male voice on the phone, for $49.99 a month your first three months, after which a slightly less discounted rate would resume, but you're welcome to cancel at any time or call back to inquire about new offers.

While Mark was supervising the cable guy, I was supervising a resident on how to place a central line. A central line is a port inserted into the jugular to draw or infuse fluid, and as I was explaining this to my residents, in the span of ten or so minutes, Mark had sent me a series of texts, most of which were sentence fragments nested in their own little speech bubble that kept vibrating my phone.

The guy from Spectrum agrees with me.

About the visibility glare,

Should we keep the TV on the west facing wall.

But here's the other problem.

The cable line is black.

While the baseboards are white.

So, to run a line discreetly

Will be hard.

I stopped reading after that and put the phone back in my pocket, on silent. I told the resident about to place the line what she needed to do in steps. She was the eager type and always nodding, but I never knew how much was being processed per nod. I asked if she had any questions. No questions, nope, she said, still nodding. Then before step one could happen, she dropped the sterile needle onto the sterile drape and the needle rolled off the drape onto the unsterile floor. Then in trying to catch the needle midair with both hands, she also dropped the ultrasound probe used to find the vein.

It's okay, I said, thinking of my strawberry bagel experience after Madeline's hug. These things happen. It's okay.

Embarrassed, the resident kept apologizing and touching her face with gloved hands that already had yellow residue. I told her to stop doing both and to go change her gloves. By the time I could check my phone again, my screen was covered in texts from Mark.

So, which wall is it?

Your call but the guy's on the clock.

Five minutes later came the last series of texts.

Decided to move the TV to the east facing wall

Because of glare,

Which came in at full force, while we

Were standing around.

But to hide the cable, we've wrapped it

In white painter's tape and fastened it to your baseboard,

Like so.

He sent me a picture.

———

ONE NIGHT I FLIPPED through the two hundred channels just to see. All sorts of shows were playing: cooking and baking shows, house-decorating programs, in-home shopping, the local news, the international news, the Weather Channel, talk shows, game shows, reality-based shows about single people trying to find love, about single women who become crazy wives, crazy wives in every city, shows about families with twenty kids, families who just clip coupons, and families who never throw anything away.

Cable was, as Mark had predicted, relaxing, and I found that there was nothing I couldn't watch, except for prime-time medical dramas in which the protagonist was always a rogue doctor who ran up alongside gurneys, then tried to reform (tear down) the health system. The rogue doctors usually looked like Reese and, as if worried that the audience or their in-show colleagues would forget, kept reminding all of us that they were doctors.

———

WE'RE HEADING TO VAIL, Fang said abruptly. He had called the morning after their Winter Bash to announce that in a few days' time they were all going on holiday and for most of next month. Colorado was, in Fang's opinion, the most beautiful state. Our mother won't be skiing, but at least she can get some fresh mountain air. They had chosen a lodge and skiing village with out-of-this-world amenities, and they themselves would be staying in a private cottage with Jacuzzis, plural.

I don't suppose you want to come, he asked. To ski or sit with our mother since the aide had been given the weeks off. I suppose you have to work through the month to avoid spending any time with us.

I said he wasn't being fair.

Am I wrong?

No, I said, but this wasn't necessarily just about right versus wrong.

There is right and there is wrong, he said, in the same tone that he used to talk about profits, about gain and loss.

I told him about my raise, hoping that once he heard this piece of news, he would be more content.

But is your title the same? he asked.

It was.

Ask for a real promotion next time. Tell your director that he either promotes you or you walk. Be more aggressive.

Berating is love, and here I was at thirty-six, still being loved.

He asked why I was always so indifferent.

Not my intention, I said, just how my voice, tone, and in-person facial expressions seemed to come across.

I didn't like the word *indifferent* either. It was just two letters off from the word that I hate.

My brother launched into a series of loaded questions, which was another technique he used to wear his recipient down. Did my indifference to a title change link back to my refusal to start a private practice, and did that link back to my refusal to leave a chaotic city for a place with more comfort and space? Did my inability to take any time off stem from either a lack of belief in my own self-worth or a masochistic nature? Or both. Because my brother has never been able to pronounce that word perfectly, he said, instead, *math statistics*.

Was I a math statistic?

But Fang pushed on.

You need to advocate more for yourself.

You need to do this and that.

Negotiation 101: If a person doesn't ask, she won't receive.

All this being said, he still found my overall problem to be one of perspective. I didn't view success in the same way he or Tami did and I didn't care for the outward appearance of it, even though maintaining a facade, however superficial, was essential to moving up. Why I couldn't grasp these points had something to do with my attitude, he believed, that I found any sign of wealth repulsive. I *chóu fù*—ed them, a verb that means "to hate the rich."

I don't *chóu fù* anyone, I said.

Tami feels the same way.

She *chóu fù*s you too?

She thinks you don't respect our progress, that you don't engage with us on the right level and you downplay everything we've worked for.

Again, not everything Fang said was wrong.

In his concluding remarks, he emphasized that if he didn't care about me, nothing I did would ever matter to him. But if he didn't voice his concerns, then who would? I was part of this family and he simply wanted to see me do well. So, when they returned from Colorado, he expected some things to change. You're coming to see us more. You're coming for Chinese New Year. Nonnegotiable.

———

SOMEWHERE OUT THERE IS a video of this amoeba eating its meal. Magnified four hundred times and at double speed, the appendages of the amoeba begin to extend and to encircle a jumpy paramecium. The large and translucent appendages touch as fingers do, thumb to index. A-OK, this amoeba says as its fingers fatten, shrinking the small circle of space until the paramecium is absorbed. Talking to my brother could feel a little like that. Me, the paramecium; him, the amoeba.

———

AS A TEAM, MY parents had worked well together. My mother was better with big picture, long term; my father was able to think through daily affairs. He would leave notes for her around the house to turn off lights, to jiggle the toilet knob when it wouldn't stop running, to always use the security chain when he wasn't home. He kept all our passports and important documents in one place. He placed her and his reading glasses on either side of their bed.

Text from Mother: Can't find my reading glasses. Don't remember where I put them.

Try the bathrooms.

Tried all the bathrooms.

Use your second pair.

That was my second pair.

Phone call from Mother: We're about to leave for the airport soon and I can't find my passport. I can't find my green card.

Nightstand?

Why would I put something like that in there?

Can you look in your nightstand?

Loud rustling. The phone is set down, picked back up.

Did you find them?

But how am I supposed to know if this is my passport?

Is your name on it?

I can't find my reading glasses.

The lodge has too many fireplaces, she wrote after they'd made it to the airport, barely, boarded the plane as the last ones, flown five hours, deboarded, and checked in. And they're too tall, these fireplaces, they're taller than me.

Did you see me take my blood pressure medication this morning?

I said I did not. Because I couldn't have.

Tami said she saw me take them, but I don't think I did. Did I mention to you about taking them?

I said she had not.

Did I turn off the lights?

The lights?

I'm in the lodge now, but I don't know if I turned off the lights back in my room. Tami said I did, but should I go back and check?

———

NEW YEAR'S EVE SERVICE. My entire team wore party hats, and when midnight hit, some of us twirled our fingers and said a woo-hoo.

Resolutions?

Older nurse: Yeah, the completion of my divorce. Moments before the young nurse announced that she'd recently gotten engaged.

Oh, hon, congrats, said the older nurse. Don't mind what I just said. The divorce was going better than she'd expected.

My parents weren't superstitious, but my paternal grandparents were and on occasion my father would indulge me with something out of Chinese lore. I knew the year 2020 to be particularly inauspicious. The earliest of Chinese calendars followed a sixty-year cycle, a sexagenary cycle, of which the thirty-seventh year was one of extremely bad luck. On the thirty-seventh year of previous cycles: 1840, start of the First Opium War against Britain; 1900, Boxer Rebellion; 1960, continuation of the Great Famine and the Great Leap Forward, during which millions of Chinese died of starvation and my father was still a young boy. Then in his teenage years, starting in 1966, came the decade-long revolution.

What revolution? I'd ask.

What revolution, he would say but not name it by name.

(*Wén gé,* of which *wén* is culture and *gé* is to remove, like to remove the skin of an animal in the process of tanning hide.)

My father wasn't a good motivator or comforter, and I wasn't a child who had been buoyed along by praise. But when we still lived under the same roof, he would sometimes say to me, I know what you're made of, daughter, because I know myself. Mettle. Grit. Wherever my father was now, I hoped that he hadn't forgotten his steel.

—

JANUARY WAS WELLNESS MONTH at the hospital, and HR sent us daily reminders to take time for lunch, to join a small group for free afternoon yoga. We were sent meditation packets, samples of chamomile tea, and email surveys about our health. Do you feel physically able to work? Do you feel mentally fit to work? On a scale of one to ten, what is your level of well? I found the last question confusing. Was ten the well or one? Because for patients there was a similar scale: in every exam room a series of cartoon faces morphed from happy to sad, from one to ten for pain and well on that scale was a one, while ten was exceedingly not.

Before the monthlong dedication took hold, it had been wellness week. Before that it had just been a day. I didn't mind Wellness Wednesday or Week; I found the alliteration catchy.

But wellness month had no alliteration, and given the slow trend toward more, wellness year was next.

What was wellness anyway? Was it anything like Loch Ness, like a seemingly placid lake with an unknowable monster hiding inside?

The seminars throughout the month focused on nutrition and healthy eating, ergonomics and injury prevention, stress management versus productivity. I saw the director at the last one, in the very back; his mouth hung open as if he were watching a bad magic show. Put your workers' productivity into a black hat and watch it disappear. Put your own productivity into a box, now saw it in half.

For a week, Reese became the center of gossip. He had been scheduled to work that week but failed to show up. Difficult poetry went unattended for a morning, acute chaos followed, and a temporary attending had to step in. Madeline and I tried to call Reese, but no response. We emailed him and no away message had been set up. The director even swung by the shared office, just to look around.

Has no one been keeping tabs on him? he asked. How does Doctor Baby-Blue Eyes just disappear?

The mystery was solved when HR informed the director, who then informed us, that Reese had requested and been approved for a wellness break that would extend to the end of January. The director was told only after the fact, because, with both mental health and disability, an employer shouldn't and couldn't meddle. These breaks were built into our contracts to be taken anytime from anywhere. A perk of the job that I never thought people actually used.

As I was leaving one evening, so was the director, and we

crossed paths in the atrium long after its café had closed. The collar of his coat was inside out, his snow boot shoelaces were untied. I asked why he was still here so late when someone of his caliber could leave as early as 4:00 p.m. My wife, he said. She was visiting her sister for a few days upstate, and whenever that happened and he was on his own, he could stay at work for however long he liked. It reminded him of his younger days, and he relished that. Then he asked me, not necessarily as my boss, he clarified, but as one concerned colleague for another, if Reese was all right, and had he been acting strange before he requested the leave. Did he say anything to you about me?

The director avoided making eye contact. I heard footsteps around us, but it was just one security guard pacing and another walking over to throw a soda can away.

I said Reese had seemed sensitive lately, but he'd always been pretty sensitive.

Would he, for instance, file a complaint?

Complaint, sir?

Against me to HR.

For?

Being too harsh.

The director was still avoiding eye contact and had hoisted his left leg up on a side ledge to tie his laces. When he bent down, he groaned. Like that of a T.rex, his head was too large for his frame and he had disproportionately short arms.

I said Reese and HR did have a special bond that I never liked to ask about or get too involved in, but in practice, I didn't see what was so scary about HR, the department seemed decently run and staffed by competent people. HR wasn't nearly as bad as the IRB, which was our internal board of review, or ethics board. Any kind of human research, any consult with or blood draw from a study subject, had to pass through them, and while HR was ever present, almost omniscient, no one really knew how the IRB worked or who worked there, much like the IRS.

The director said both departments were overregulated, but HR more so in that they could involve themselves in your personal life.

I said, I've never had a problem with them.

But once they find a discrepancy, game over. Never give them a shred of doubt.

Doubt about what?

The director finally straightened up and looked me in the eye. He put a finger to his lip, though I never knew him to be paranoid.

I said if he was worried, then should I be? A few weeks ago, I'd taken a page out of the director's own phonaesthetics book and told Reese how a hypothetical woman might tell a hypothetical man to fuck right off.

The director's mouth twitched; his pupils became two black dots on two white spheres. You what? Fuck right off and not just fuck off? But that could send someone over the edge, couldn't it? A person who was already unsteady.

He seemed fine with it, actually, I said. He didn't know what I meant.

Even worse, replied the director.

We stood near the exit doors of the atrium, far enough that they wouldn't open automatically but close enough that we could see the breath of the people walking outside.

Oh well, he said, out of our hands now, it is what it is, and the cards will fall as they may. When the director resorted to idioms, I knew he was at his linguistic limit. What's the opposite of kill two birds with one stone? he asked me.

I said, Huh?

The opposite. As in we're the two birds that might have killed a third one with our stones.

I explained that birds can do lots of things that humans can't, like fly, but birds can't pick up stones and throw them like projectiles, so no such idiom exists.

The lack of a perfect English phrase for our predicament seemed to frustrate him and the director made a *grr* sound.

———

IF I WAS IN my apartment, the television was on. I didn't always watch, but the sounds of people talking at low volume were nice, soothing, even if it was for seemingly an hour of commercials.

When I finally heard the name Jerry, I came out from the kitchen where I'd been waiting for water to boil, to pour into my Cup Noodles. On-screen, I saw a short funny-looking man call a tall funny-looking man Jerry. George and Jerry. They were in Jerry's apartment, and then right on cue, another tall funny-looking man with fluffy hair, in an oversized plaid shirt, barged in. He had a shaky way of moving and talking and, out of the three, seemed to have mismanaged his nerves the most. Something funny was said by Jerry, then George, then Kramer. The laugh track played and played.

More booklets came for me in the mail. Several vacation catalogs for ski resorts (to the mountains!) and all-inclusive tropical escapes (book now, why wait!).

A magazine called *Awake!* The header said that a stress-free life is possible. Subheaders and the first page: What causes stress? Divorce, death, illness, crime, job loss, natural disasters, the hectic pace of life. How to deal with stress. One, don't hold two handfuls of work. Two, kill your stress with kindness. Sixteen pages.

The thickest of silken envelopes would soon arrive for me as well. Tomato red, fiery red, the red of oxygen-rich blood. I noticed the postmark date for this invite was weeks ago, so it must have gotten delayed. Time of the bash was set in two weeks, at the end of Spring Festival Golden Week on February 1.

It was soon to be the year of the rat and an embroidered piece of the invite explained what the coming zodiac year entailed. Men born in the year of the rat are curious, handy, and adaptive to new environments. Women born in the year of the rat are organized, neat, and place a great value on family life. Notable people who are rats: *fútbol* superstar Cristiano Ronaldo, basketball all-star LeBron James, and the Great One, Wayne Gretzky. Please join us at our home to celebrate history, family, and the importance of coming together.

I wondered why Fang stopped there. He could have continued to list notable people born in the year of the rat. It took only a minute of googling on my part to find more.

Civil rights activist Rosa Parks.

Computer scientist Alan Turing.

Former president Richard Nixon.

The world's first cloned mammal, Dolly the Sheep.
Dad.

———

AT THE END OF DECEMBER, some people in China, in the city of Wuhan, had contracted pneumonia, a cluster of cases stemming from a visit to a fish market earlier that month. Cases continued throughout January, and details about them were scarce. Except that it turned out not to be pneumonia and to be a new kind of disease, from an unknown virus, possibly derived from bats that were being sold illegally at the market. I didn't know whether I should be paying attention or not. I'd never been to Wuhan and was no virologist. My mother hadn't texted me about it, nor my brother. The local news touched on it briefly and went straight into weather and traffic delays. The international news spent a minute longer on China and then moved to turmoil in the Middle East.

But viruses have always fascinated me, and I couldn't look at a New York skyline without thinking of them. The water towers on many buildings reminded me of bacteriophages, or viruses that infect bacteria, with a capsid-bound head and legs that can attach themselves to the host and force entry. Fascinating to me that viruses could infect living cells and take over, but not be living themselves. Only carriers of genetic code, only genes bound by membrane. Not being alive means that viruses are ungovernable by evolutionary laws like survival of the fittest or reproductive strength. So, without this basic constraint and purpose, how have they persisted through millennia, invading cell after cell? Plagues, the outcomes are always bad for animals, for humans, but viruses themselves are neither good nor bad. They have no moral compass or desire to live, and so the only reason I had for their existence was random chance.

——

ON FRIDAY, JANUARY 17, at around 3:00 p.m., the time our office seemed to have the most visitors, a woman I'd never met came in and asked if she could have a few moments of my time. Another attending was here, but she was on the other side of the room, wearing large, noise-canceling headphones that looked like earmuffs and plowing through her emails at a hundred words a minute.

Where should I sit? the woman asked, and I gestured to Reese's empty chair. Reese had a messy desk that I tried not to look at. Pens were scattered everywhere and papers fanned out, brown rings where coffee mugs used to be. Some of his shelving had collapsed yesterday, over his desk and keyboard. Against my advice, he had stuck them to the wall with Command strips instead of real screws.

The woman took notice and said the desk was in violation of several health codes, hinging on unsafe.

My co-worker is not well, I said.

Who? She asked and after I told her, she wrote a note to herself, on a small spiral notebook, that she had in her black blazer pocket.

I asked if she was a detective. Had Reese perished on vacation and an ongoing investigation been started?

She said no, not a detective, and that my office mate who, in the workplace, should be more correctly referred to as Dr.

Mayhew, was doing better. Like all of us with respect to well-ness, he was taking it one day at a time.

But I'm not here to discuss Dr. Mayhew, she continued, and produced from her black tote a manila folder that had my full name, first and last, handwritten on the tab. I'd watched enough television now to know. Appearance of a mysterious blazered woman was never good, compounded with your name on a tab was worse. But I was taken aback that employee records were still being kept manually, that this folder, my folder, had been filled in and written on, then put into a physi-cal cabinet to be plucked out for today, and that there were still cabinets around and not supercooled rooms with banks of supercooled processors.

I asked the woman about all this.

We're HR, she said, not *Mission Impossible*.

I laughed, because this time I got the reference. I'd seen one of those movies, I said. Disavowed. Crazy stunts. *Boom, bam, pow*.

She smiled at me, but it was an uncomfortable smile, like she knew something I didn't and wasn't looking forward to what was ahead. Then she opened my file and started to read from it. It was my CV and certifications, a short paragraph of biographical information.

You have a brother in Greenwich, parents in Shanghai, though your father recently passed, our most sincere condo-lences.

I tilted my head and asked how she'd heard about that.

About what?

My father.

It's stated here in your file.

But how did it get in my file? I hadn't told HR in any official capacity; I hadn't updated any biographical information
since I was hired.

She straightened the papers in my file. Now the four sheets
of paper were perfectly stacked.

Is this information incorrect? she asked.

I said no.

Then she didn't see the issue. The woman's eyes were uneven, in that one sat slightly higher than the other. Her cheeks
had a layer of fine peach fuzz.

Recently we processed your raise, she said. Thank you for
your hard work and dedication to our hospital. Your director
deeply respects and advocates for you. He has identified you as
a must-keep personnel, so we will do our best.

But, the woman continued, when we processed your raise,
we did notice some inconsistencies. For instance, we noticed
that after visiting China for two days last September, you resumed work that immediate Monday.

The director's paranoia became my own, and my mind
jumped to whether this woman was here to punish me for having taken an unsanctioned trip to a foreign land. I'd learned
about the McCarthy era in school and how ever since the words
*communism* and *red* have become synonymous with China and
its people. Some patients liked to know if I was born here, if
English was my first language, and I worried that this woman
was here to ask the third follow-up question that those patients
never thought of but an unsolicited mailing from a random
Asian cultural center had: Still, despite being born here and
fluent, were you ever part of the CCP, and if so, do you plan to
quit?

Visiting China is now okay, I stated, stiffening my back and imagining myself, as the doorman had taught me, in the center of an elevator going up. Borders are open and international relations, at least superficially, are not awful. But had I forgotten to submit a travel form to them or to the internal board of review?

She said it wasn't that, and I could visit China as much as I liked. Neither HR nor the IRB was the TSA.

A toss-up, who had more power in this hospital, HR or the IRB or accounts payable, though each group would probably name itself. Had I ever met an IRB or an accounts payable employee? No. And this was the closest I'd ever been to any HR personnel.

I asked if her coming today had anything to do with Wuhan.

Wuhan?

I stayed in Shanghai and nowhere else, I said. I explained that the two cities are far apart and as different as Omaha and Manhattan. Wuhan being Omaha, an inland city filled with nice midwestern people who took on industry jobs and believed in a hard day's work. It isn't their fault, I said abruptly, about the situation now developing there.

She raised her eyebrows and asked which situation was I referring to?

The fish market, the bats.

She repeated the word *bats,* then looked down at my folder. There's nothing here about bats, she said. Or fish markets. She closed the folder and looked back at me with a new kindness. Our main concerns for you are less global, should we say, and more focused. Our concerns are twofold and with that she held up two fingers like the peace sign or like *V* for victory. The first, that from mid-October to now, a period of almost twelve weeks, I'd taken no full weeks off. Attendings must take off-service weeks, or else the workflow in the community becomes imbalanced. The second, that I had resumed work right after my China trip, a personal trip of great importance, a pilgrimage effectively to bid goodbye to my father, and had not taken the recommended one month leave of bereavement.

Bereavement?

A person only has one father.

I said I was aware.

Then were you not aware of the leave? It's been a great initiative for our senior staff members with aging parents. We believe that even most well-seasoned health professionals should grieve.

I did know about the leave, I said, but thought it was optional.

The woman smiled at me again, but it could have also been a grimace. Despite her uneven eyes, she had one of those perfectly level mouths, of which the corners didn't turn up or down.

Strictly speaking the leave was optional, as she explained, and could be waived for distant relatives, an aunt or uncle, a second cousin. But immediate family made up our core supports, our pillars, and those deep in grief, more or less lost in it, often don't know how to feel about the death unless they take the full course of treatment.

I clarified that she was talking about bereavement and not an infection.

Bereavement is a wound, she said.

It was, but mine had healed. I'd worked through it already.

The woman took out a small tin of mints from her other blazer pocket and ate one. She didn't offer me any mints and slid the tin back. In case it wasn't clear, your month off would be compensated, and at your new elevated rate. You would simply be flagged as unavailable in the system. The time is meant for you to spend however you wish.

I said I wanted to be available at all hours. I felt that giving in to this request was giving in to pity, and my father wouldn't have approved. He would have reminded me that there's no such thing as a free lunch.

We see this a lot, actually, said the woman, crossing her legs. Doctors who refuse to rest as if it were a sign of weakness, but it's not. Stopping momentarily to reassess, recenter, release— the three *R*s—is actually a sign of strength.

I asked what would happen if I forwent bereavement.

Technically, nothing, she said, but we cannot guarantee absolutely nothing down the line. No one has refused leave once it's been suggested, so should you pursue this path, you would be the first.

Beneath the blazer, the woman wore a yellow blouse that was stretched so tightly across her chest it reminded me of a cushion.

We are not trying to inconvenience you, said Yellow Cushion. We are only trying to help. Compared with other hospitals of our caliber, our attendings report being the most fulfilled. Research has shown that healthy attendings do better work and are protected from the forces of pettiness, internal competition, and deindividualization. This time is our gift to you.

Consider it the hospital's way of reaching its arms out and giving you a hug.

—

MY LEAVE IN TOTAL would be six weeks, and that included the one month of bereavement along with two off-service weeks to make up for the many I had forgone. The leave was to start immediately on Monday, January 20, through all of February and the first week of March. Before Yellow Cushion left, she handed me a notice sheet with these logistical details bulleted out, including which attendings would be covering for me on each of the six weeks. The sheet was so unambiguous and well organized that it reminded me of one of my own handouts and I couldn't get too mad. Then Madeline came in to pack up for the day and asked why I was just sitting there, holding a piece of paper and not facing my monitor again. I glanced at her. I didn't reply.

Is it your mom? she asked. Oh my gosh, did she? Both parents back to back?

I said my mother was fine.

But your face, said Madeline. You look gray.

I felt gray, I said.

Doctors complained to each other all the time and to anyone else who would listen. The system is broken. Referring mostly to bureaucracy, insurance, the skyrocketing cost of care, Big Pharma's focus on only lucrative drugs, the cost of medical training itself plus licensing, and the exorbitant salaries of some specialties like oncology. But who could have broken our own system if not us? And the system wasn't so much broken as it was circuitous, self-blaming, and operating under false pretenses. A hospital is a business, and businesses like to make money whether that profit came from goods or the extension of human lives.

The medical system wasn't perfect because no system is perfect, but I still admired it for being a hierarchical masterpiece of specialized skill. Moreover, how could a system be that flawed if it had allowed someone like me in?

Was I? I might've been—having my own moment of peak sadness like each of my residents and like Reese. But whereas they felt the training had stifled their personhoods, I relished that feeling of anonymity and of being a cog in the whole. So, what I was experiencing now was perhaps the reverse crisis, from having been repudiated by the group to be on my own. I could hear my father asking, What's the plan, doctor-daughter, what's the plan? I could feel the totally panicked doctor-daughter realizing she had no plan nor six weeks' worth of person-y things to do.

When I continued to say nothing, Madeline felt my forehead and said I was a little warm. She plucked the notice from my hands and started to read.

Are you bereaved? she asked from behind the page, her eyes scanning line by line at an increasing pace.

I said I couldn't be sure anymore. This all seemed too surreal.

Madeline then replied, slowly and softly, that she couldn't lose me as well. Me and Reese. She couldn't be on this side of the office alone after already committing to us as colleagues. When Madeline finally set the notice down, there was a look in her eyes, like that of a frantic gerbil about to go for a perilous sprint on a wheel. She knelt and turned my chair to face her. She expressed regret for what she was going to do, but she had to get her agitation out somehow and asked me not to take it to heart.

Madeline, I said, as a warning. Madeline, hang on, we can get you a stress ball.

But it was already too late.

When your feet can't dangle off the seat, flying can feel a lot like sitting. When your armrests are being shaken by a co-worker, sitting can feel a little like flying.

As the entire chair rocked, I was back on that plane with my grainy apple slices. It was comforting at first, the rattling of all my limbs, the sloping around of my cheeks, the confusion as my brain sloshed in its own fluid like pickled vegetables in a jar, but eventually, I had to ask Madeline to stop shaking me and my chair. I was already nauseated.

My last resort was to head into the director's office without a scheduled appointment. He was in the same position as before, seated at his desk, the view behind him the same set of bridges and cars, planes landing and taking off. He glanced away from his computer at me and seemed startled, as if he'd seen a ghost.

What are you doing here? he whispered. You're supposed to be on leave.

Tomorrow.

He nodded solemnly and asked if there was anything he could still do for me. Nespresso? A handshake?

I asked to stay and he said that decision was out of his hands.

But what if I never told anyone and just never left. I could order a sleeping bag and store it under my desk. Shower with wet wipes.

They'll make an example out of you, he said.

How? I asked. It wasn't possible to make an example out of a model minority.

The director doubted it too but still urged me not to take any chances. What HR frequently said to them, the directors, about the proper running of a hospital: if you do not respect the corporate form, the corporate form will not respect you. He repeated this with a shudder.

Good news is that it's just six weeks, he said. Go see your family. Go to Greenwich. Take naps, walks. Time will fly.

I couldn't quite picture that, time flying six weeks or forty-two days at a time, unless I was put into a coma.

And when you come back, which you will, all this will be behind you and I'll prioritize you for any shift you want.

I thanked him for his continued and unwavering support.

He said it was the least he could do.

Then I said something that surprised even myself.

Director, the first time I put on my white coat, it felt like home. From having moved around so much and with no child-hood or ancestral home to return to, I didn't think myself capable. I didn't prioritize home or comfort, because if everyone did, then immigrants like my parents, brother, and sister-in-law couldn't exist. Home was not a viable concept for them until later, and it wasn't a concept for me until the day I put on that coat, this coat. I pulled at my white lapel to show him. From then on, I knew that my occupation would become my home. To have a home is a luxury, but I now understand why people attach great value to it and are loyal to defend it. Home is where you fit in and take up space.

My director rubbed his eyes. He said he was touched by what I said and insisted on shaking my hand.

His campfire-for-hair secretary had come to the door already, had lightly tapped to say that his next appointment was here, and without realizing, I'd extended my hand forward toward some invisible flame. Bending over his desk to shake my hand with vigor, the director said that while we still had to follow protocol, once I was back in full force he would put my face and those words on a brochure. Because if I could feel at home in this hospital, then more physicians like me would come.

I spent my last hour at the hospital with ECMO and pushed its cart to a window overlooking Morningside Park.

This park has seen changes, I told ECMO. My doorman says that just ten years ago, no one went into this park past dusk alone. There were areas shrouded from view by overgrown trees and shrubbery. Long stretches of bumpy asphalt, twisted metal fencing, and sudden cliffs, playgrounds with no kids and gunshots heard at night. But in recent years, an immaculate green lawn was put in, a new baseball diamond, a kidney-shaped pond with turtles, floodlights at night for safety. In summer, the park was nice to run through, and when I first moved here, I had taken a few jogs, up into the secluded terraces that at a certain point opened up to a sprawling view of the city.

ECMO, I said, you would love it. It's tidal volume, that view.

Tidal volume is about half a liter. It's the amount of air in a single breath taken at rest. How to remember this term, I had written in my handouts, is to imagine yourself sitting on a beach. The beach is empty and the sand is clean. You watch the tides roll in, tides that are controlled by the moon, that big rock orbiting us out in space. You put your chin on your knee and inhale, exhale. This is the kind of quiet breath we mean.

———

MY BEREAVEMENT DAYS BEGAN with television, alternating between local news, the weather, the home shopping network, cooking competitions, and daytime television that played reruns of old sitcoms and shows about nothing.

Kramer barges in, takes out from Jerry's fridge half a pound of deli meat, two slices of thick bread, and makes himself a sandwich. After taking one bite of the sandwich, he spits the bite out. Too mushy. Leaves the sandwich there on the counter and barges out.

Kramer eats a chocolate cupcake. He writes the word *cupcake* down on a small slip of paper that will be his running tab at Jerry's apartment and that will now allow Kramer to take whatever he wants.

Jerry calls Kramer "Hobo Joe."

Is this your half can of soda in the fridge? says Jerry, holding up the can in question.

No, no, says Kramer. It's yours. My half is gone.

Daytime television transitioned into prime-time movies. Action movies, superhero movies, horror, romantic comedies, and the classics. Or what commercials promised to be a classic.

An empty New York City street, under the light fog of

dawn, gray and blue buildings rising up all around, monolith-like, and down this empty street, down Fifth Avenue, comes an old, boxy yellow cab. Out steps a tall and slim woman, black dress, gloves, and sunglasses, a long white scarf with fringe, and reams of pearls draped across her neckline and back. Idyllic music plays, a lush violin, many violins, an oboe, a choir, as this stunning pearled-up woman peruses those curtained window displays of that famed jewelry store, Tiffany's, while eating a croissant. Inside the store hang large chandeliers, heavy with crystals, draped in the same way as the pearls around her neck, because the woman herself is a chandelier, a fixture and an object.

Holly Golightly is a runaway orphan turned call girl, and being at Tiffany's calms her down. She talks about the quietness and the proud look of the place, how nothing bad could ever happen to you in there. She says, If I could find a real-life place that makes me feel like Tiffany's, then I'd buy some furniture and give the cat a name.

Proud, quiet (on a slow day), how nothing bad could ever happen to you there (under the right care). Which was I bereaved of? The temporary loss of the hospital or the permanent loss of my father?

Here was a fatherless girl in the big city, in an almost empty apartment with a nameless cat.

Here was a fatherless girl in the big city, in an almost empty apartment with a robot vacuum.

A fact demonstrated by so many movies and shows—and this Oscar-nominated classic was no exception—was that you could not live in Manhattan without having at least one crazy neighbor.

Holly has a crazy neighbor who is made up to be Japanese, but the actor himself is not Japanese, and this incongruence gave me pause, though I wasn't exactly sure why, except that by the end, I didn't like what I was watching. I didn't like the neighbor or my confusion around him. Mr. Yunioshi has exaggerated facial expressions, a grotesque way of baring all his teeth, spitting while he speaks, and mispronouncing every other word. Was this how people saw my father? And how people saw me? Because someone like me could never be Holly, of course. Only in my mind could I be her, but to the rest of the world, I was a Mr. Yunioshi or a Mr. Yunioshi's daughter.

Suppose Mr. Yunioshi's daughter did exist and had been fine on her own, living alone and unperturbed, until one day a Kramer moved in across the hall. Would that make good television? Would anyone want to watch?

At first, my version of Kramer still knocked, before transitioning full time to the spare key, which was now fastened to his key ring with a white label that said JOAN. I would hear my lock barrel turn and then Mark would be in my living room.

He only brought food over and never took it. Homemade pies both sweet and savory, breakfast muffins, loaves of sourdough bread. Whatever he brought that we couldn't finish, he would expertly wrap in cellophane and stick in the fridge for me to eat later.

He had more furniture pieces for me, old stuff that he didn't need anymore, or new stuff he had bought on a whim but didn't need. He blamed online shopping for being too easy. Not only were there so many deals, sales, cash back promotions, but with just a few clicks of your mouse, a rug could appear for you in a matter of days.

He did have a rug for me, as well as an ottoman, a marble side table for Suede Chair, a bin of kitchen utensils, a large woodblock chopping board, and an assortment of fridge magnets.

My fridge now had five magnets, one of which was a tap-dancing baguette that had the word PAIN on it in all caps and red type font. When I pointed to the dancing baguette magnet and said, Pain, he frowned. It's pronounced *paan,* he said, his mouth in the shape of a flat oval. It's French for "bread."

While making room for my new lapis-glazed stoneware dinner plates that he'd bought in bulk by accident during a flash sale, he looked through my many cabinets of flavored sparkling water, from tangerine to pamplemousse. He picked up one can and skimmed the nutritional label on the back.

How is that possible, he asked, for *flavored* water to have zero calories? Shouldn't the *flavor* have some calories? How could a *flavor* additive not?

I said the flavor was just an essence and essences didn't have calories.

But if I'm able to taste it, then shouldn't it have some calories?

Your body can't digest essence, and whatever isn't digested, technically, has no calories. Steel, for instance—say you ate an entire steel bar, your mouth would be able to taste the steel and your brain would say not a good idea, but since your body doesn't metabolize steel, no calories there.

Is that really how it works? he asked.

I confirmed again.

That's not how it really works, he decided.

More books. To add to the stalagmite by Suede Chair and

new mini stalagmites along the wall. These were books that he'd recently finished and thought I would like.

Ever read him? Mark asked, showing me a thick volume of essays by a world-renowned brain surgeon. Not bad, he said of the book. Verbose in lots of places, the middle is a slog, and the ending wasn't quite earned, but otherwise brilliant. Taught me a little more about your kind.

I said I wasn't a brain surgeon.

He rolled his eyes and said that he knew. Just a little joke.

Mark could provoke with jokes or without them, and now that he was always in my apartment and felt comfortable enough around me, he liked to provoke me into having conversations with him that I didn't want to have.

What do you have against rogue doctors anyway? he'd asked after I'd refused to watch with him an old episode of *ER*.

The point of the training is to un-rogue you, I'd said. To prevent the hero, savior, God complex so that a doctor doesn't break team. Else who would trust her again? A hospital is an ecosystem, not a pedestal.

Mark could see where I was coming from, but just to bat for the other side (which he did a lot), just for the sake of discussion, hear me out for a second, he would add. There was still something noble and sacrificial in what I did, even though I as one doctor, one data point, downplayed my role. While I didn't do all the procedures myself, I drew up the plan. The idea generation and oversight made me the lead person, the architect. Do we credit the Eiffel Tower to Alexandre-Gustave Eiffel or the construction workers who built it?

By construction workers, I asked, do you mean the nurses,

interns, residents, techs, the janitorial staff who clean and disinfect daily, the cafeteria staff who feed us, teams of engineers who keep our database and lifesaving machines running?

He said let's agree to disagree, for now.

A greeting he insisted on using with me was What's up, Doc? Then as he was leaving, Later, Doc. When I asked if he could stop calling me Doc, he said I should consider it a term of endearment and no can do, Doc.

Since I started staying at home, a daily query from him was why I was home so much now, when before he would be lucky to see me once every other week.

I deflected the question for a while but eventually told him about my leave. To simplify matters, I chose to not mention my father. Mark didn't need to know about him and I was tired of explaining that he'd lived in China, where the rest of my family was from, but not me.

Six weeks? Mark said. That's a lot of time off, isn't it? Most jobs don't even give you half as much. He thought docs worked around the clock.

I said a month of it was mandated.

On what grounds?

I said I'd forgotten to complete a training, and, by the time I'd remembered, my window had expired. I was making up these lies as we went along.

What kind of training? Mark asked.

The first word that came to me was *wellness*. A training about wellness with lots of different modules, both in person and online.

For a light afternoon snack, Mark had made us a charcuterie board of aged crystalized gouda and *paan*. He chewed his gouda slowly and pensively, while I went through several cubes at once.

But why would they give you more time off for not doing something? he asked. Isn't vacation sort of a reward? So, shouldn't they have made you do the training anyway, then assigned you more work?

All good points, ones that I hadn't considered before I decided to lie, hence why the general guideline is to not.

I said yeah, weird, isn't it, but that's just how things were done. Our hospital was a peculiar one, with its own rules and regulations. It could have also been a miscommunication between the departments; either way it was a decision that I had to respect. When Mark posed more questions, I shrugged and said I didn't want to talk about it anymore. I prided myself on finishing all of my trainings on time and to not have done one made me sad.

That was what I'd assumed until the following day, when after he'd let himself in and called me doc, he brought up my leave and made-up training again.

Having reconsidered my unfortunate situation, he hoped that I wasn't being bullied. It happened to diligent employees all the time. A mysterious glitch in the system, and somehow, they found themselves on a long holiday, which was a euphemism for a suspension for something they didn't do.

He asked if I had been suspended, then.

I said those weren't the words that anyone had used.

Could someone have surreptitiously done this to you?

Not to my knowledge.

In the last few months, any strife at work?

I felt back in a counselor's office and a bright light had been placed on me with a slim window of response. Out of habit, I said no.

You're a woman of color in a male-dominated field and you haven't experienced any strife?

What do you mean by strife? I asked. Because in my head I was picturing labor camps and starvation. Having grown up in the streets or been born with a congenital defect, having never had a chance to prove myself or to get my education—that was strife.

Friction, discord, a dispute, he said.

Just one dispute is what you mean by strife?

For sure. But can also be multiple disputes around a central issue.

There hadn't been many disputes, I replied. My director and I got along. My team and I got along. One colleague had offered to save me her eggs; another had shown me how to juggle. I left some parts out, like when Madeline had shaken my chair, and when Reese had thrown three foam stress balls for me to catch but almost pelted me instead. None of these felt quite like strife, but quirks. Everyone had their quirks, and who was I to judge?

What do you mean by central issue? I asked, which I shouldn't have, because it launched Mark into a long, abstract speech filled with words that made me wince. He thought my wellness training was a sham, a ruse, and a consequence of systemic r-word, through and through. Whenever he used the r-word, my left cheek muscle would twitch and I had a desire to crack my neck.

An odd coincidence, don't you think, he asked, to mandate

an Asian doctor complete this kind of training when the hospital might've been laxer on someone else. Don't Asians have to outscore their white counterparts across the board? Don't they have to outscore other Asians and sometimes themselves?

I said, Well, yeah, but that's for everything.

And how does that make you feel?

How does outscoring someone make me feel?

(Should it have made me feel anything? Were tests about feelings or putting the right answer down on a page?)

Mark said it should make me feel cheated. Through tests or any quantitative measure of ability, Asians have already proven that they're assiduous, compliant, and competent, but then in interviews, in real workplace settings, they must also prove to their colleagues and superiors that they have some semblance of a personality, else they immediately get classified as robotic.

I wanted to put my head in my hands. Then with my head and ears covered, I wanted to walk out of my apartment and go somewhere else.

Wellness was a spectrum, my neighbor emphasized. Someone else's well might be another person's not-well. To force everyone to follow a standard set of mannerisms, set inevitably by a majority group and ruling class, was wrong. So, he couldn't help but suspect that the real purpose of my training was to discreetly check in on me and to make sure I wasn't one of those robots. He used air quotes around "robots," and I watched his fingers move up and down like rabbit ears. But could it be possible that some Asians seem stiff because of differing cultural norms and expectations? And some Asians seeming stiff doesn't mean all of them are, so if a wellness training couldn't be culturally sensitive enough to accommodate disparate starting points, then it was just another form of institutional discrimination.

The d-word caused me to flinch as well, after which I lost my train of thought. I asked, Who are we discriminating against again? The people or the robots?

He didn't give me any answers. Instead, he said that I was an incredible person. You're one of a kind, he told me. Don't ever let anyone tell you otherwise. Don't forget who you are.

———

ON JANUARY 23, WUHAN was sealed off, in the strictest meaning of the term: no one enters and no one leaves. Days before the lockdown took effect, five million people left the city without being screened. The crowds at the train station were astounding, buying tickets to go anywhere, as long as the place wasn't Wuhan.

On January 24, Chinese New Year started, a one-month holiday, and the largest annual human migration in the world, with, on average, four hundred million people traveling, three billion trips being made, thousands of train tickets sold per second, and selling out within a minute of being posted. The migration was usually from urban to rural, as some 250 million migrant workers left the cities to see their families back home.

At some point, these numbers just became numbers to me. I couldn't comprehend the size of China anymore, nor what growing up there would've been like.

I called my mother, but it went straight to voicemail. I called my brother, but he didn't pick up. I texted Tami, What's going on?

Tami replied right away that nothing was going on, everyone was just busy skiing and having fun. Your mother forgets to charge her phone sometimes. Or she accidently turns it off.

I asked Tami what she thought about the news, since all of her family were still in Chongqing, and wasn't that kind of close to Wuhan?

She replied that I clearly wasn't familiar with China's geography, and why would I be? But Chongqing was like an eleven-hour drive from Wuhan or a six-hour bullet train ride. Almost five hundred miles apart and in completely different provinces. But should there be any trouble, her family would follow government guidelines exactly and be fine.

On January 25, which was New Year's Day and officially the year of the rat, the lockdown expanded to other cities in Hubei Province, confining fifty-nine million people to their homes, or a larger population than New York City, London, Paris, and Moscow combined.

On January 25, Mark was sitting on my broken futon reading a book of poems while I was sitting in Suede Chair watching clips on my phone about the Hubei lockdown. I saw images of red electronic banners running up and down buildings that said in Chinese DO NOT GATHER THIS NEW YEAR, DO NOT CELEBRATE, REMEMBER TO WASH YOUR HANDS, and UNLESS YOU WISH DEATH UPON OTHERS, BE A GOOD CITIZEN AND STAY INSIDE.

After turning a page that was mostly blank, Mark suggested that since I was home so much now, we should revisit the idea of cohosting a get-together for the building. It could then be the entire ninth floor, both our doors would be open and guests could go back and forth. We had the same dinnerware now, the same decor sensibility.

I said I was worried about Wuhan and by extension China. I had him look at the images, and even after I translated, he didn't seem too concerned.

Yeah, but didn't the last SARS outbreak peter out? The virus mutated within a month or something. At least that's what he'd been reading online.

I said, Each virus is different, no two are alike.

Like snowflakes, he said, and I said nothing. Because a virus was nothing like a snowflake.

But we've all gotten a type of corona before, he stated. It was in the common cold, albeit a bit more severe this time. Just don't touch your T-zone, what every article seems to suggest.

He showed me these articles that he was referencing, all fact-checked, he said, by reputable sources. I scrolled through them and saw only words, predictions. Much of medicine is built on hindsight, but hindsight usually means that in exchange for knowledge a lot of people first have to die. I said whatever happened, demand could not exceed supply. I thought I was speaking calmly, until Mark pointed out that I was not.

Hey, he said.

Hey what?

Our health systems are built for this stuff.

I said they really weren't.

Let's agree to disagree, for now. And remember—he paused for some sort of effect.

Remember what?

It's on the other side of the world.

—

NO FORMAL ANTONYM FOR *catastrophizing* exists, but why did it seem that more people had this trait than not? Isn't it more evolutionary favorable to catastrophize? Does fortune truly favor the bold?

—

FOR OVER A WEEK, I didn't hear from my mother in a significant way. She had ignored my texts about why she was ignoring my calls with one-sentence replies that all was fine, and since January 23 I'd tried to call every day. I had become that daughter, the overprotective and possibly annoying kind, the daughter who believes she is also the parent to a parent who doesn't like being the child.

I could picture my mother glancing at her phone. Who's texting and calling me so much? Who's blowing up my phone? Oh, it's just Joan-na. Then turning the phone down, facedown, and resuming whatever it was that she was doing, like finishing a hot beverage. She wasn't bound to me, and besides being my mother, she was free to do other things. I'd come to realize long ago that my parents didn't fit parental norms and whether that was a result of their own personalities, genetics, or the slow grind of immigration, who could say. A normal parent calls too much, wants to be there every step of the way, and can never leave their kids alone. But that my parents could leave me alone, and separate themselves from me, did not necessarily mean that I was uncared for. We know what you're made out of, daughter, because we know ourselves. We won't always be there for you, but we trust ourselves to have raised you well.

As I gazed out the window, it started to snow.

Maybe my mother has learned to ski, I thought. Far-fetched but not impossible. A near seventy-year-old woman skiing, peacefully and idyllically, with just the sounds of her blades cutting white powder underfoot, and casually checking her ringing phone on the downhill, then putting the phone back in her coat and skiing on. But then this serene image turned scary. What if she fell and fractured her knee? She didn't have health insurance here, nor did she know the hospital system. I would need to find her a good surgeon and then convince this surgeon to let me scrub in. But because I wouldn't be able to shut my mouth while I watched, I would constantly be questioning the good surgeon and his technique until he eventually asked me to leave. With all due respect, and we appreciate you being here for your mom, but please get out of my OR.

On January 27, two days into the year of the rat, she finally picked up.

Yes? What is it? she asked. She seemed agitated and announced that their monthlong trip had come to an end, and she was trying to pack. But where were her reading glasses, passport, green card, and plastic box of pills? They were set to leave in a few hours, and no one was helping her—why wasn't anyone helping her?

I asked if she had learned to ski.

Ski? She'd hardly left the lodge.

Was the lodge fun?

Why would sitting all day in a lodge with Tami be fun?

Why would being watched by her hawk of a daughter-in-law and followed from place to place like prey be fun?

I sensed that my mother needed to vent and that I could be that for her, a blank wall against which she could throw things, as I'd seen in some movies when, to talk about something stressful, two people will play that game of aggressively hitting a tiny, hard ball indoors, side by side, with fuzzy sweatbands around their heads. I could be that game for my mother. I could be squash.

How's the scenery?

Predictable.

And the food? The hot chocolate?

Nanny makes it better.

Anything else?

What would you do in this hypothetical situation? she asked. Say hypothetically her February flight from JFK to Shanghai had been canceled because the American airline that she'd booked with had enacted a temporary China ban; pilots and flight staff were refusing to fly to that country until the Wuhan situation had been managed. She was upset about the cancellation, but Fang saw this as a chance for her to stay longer with them, maybe even through the summer months, when they could all go glamping.

She asked if I knew what that was.

I did not.

Glamorous camping. Notwithstanding how absurd that sounded, she couldn't stay here until then, she needed to get back. She had her own summer plans. Reunions with college friends, a trip to Wuxi, to Tai Lake, planned with her sisters.

Fang brought you into it, she said. He told me to ask you

whether there was any real danger to this virus or if it was the media again, scaring everyone about China. The reasoning behind the China ban had been safety precautions, and with ten thousand cases there now, two hundred deaths, she could recognize the hazard as well. But she too suspected bias. If the U.S. had this many cases or more, would they expect other countries' airlines to ban them, or would they demand to keep on traveling? Just as my brother did, she believed that if there was ever a chance to ostracize China, America would take it.

Stay, Fang had urged.

But for how long?

We'll see.

Those words had angered my mother, as had his tone— could she sense some glee in it, in finally being able to tell this old lady what to do? She felt boxed in and exasperated in the quaint mountain cottage where mother and son were having their fight.

I said the virus was real and my professional opinion she could relay back to Fang, hypothetically.

Of course it's fucking real, said my mother, shouted my mother. I wasn't born yesterday.

———

ON JANUARY 28, A large piece of card stock was stuffed into every mailbox in our building, and a pile of them was stacked neatly outside on a newspaper box. The NYC Tenant helpline: Are you a tenant who needs help? Are you being harassed by your landlord? Do you have questions about your lease? Call 311 for more information.

The very same day, my mother texted me from Eagle County Regional Airport, thirty-seven miles outside of Vail, that they were waiting to fly back to JFK, where a car would be waiting to drive them back to Greenwich. So much waiting, she wrote. Then: See you at the bash.

I'd completely forgotten.

(No, I hadn't.)

But I thought I'd completely forgotten that I was expected in Connecticut this weekend for their Chinese New Year bash. I tried to forget Fang's ultimatum again, but it was impossible to fake-forget twice. I had nothing else to do, nothing else on my mind, and when I looked at my calendar for February, it was totally blank.

———

THE BRAND OF SPARKLING water that I bought in bulk was LaCroix. But on January 30, when I went to the store to stock up, they didn't have the tangerine flavor or my other flavor of choice, pamplemousse, no orange, passion fruit, hibiscus, nothing except coconut, the flavor I liked least so was never going to buy.

Been a hiccup in the supply chain, explained the manager. And restocking could take up to a month. He suggested I try another brand, maybe Poland Spring.

I said for the sake of my family, I only bought from the French. My brother preferred L'Occitane amenities bags. My sister-in-law was in love with Celine. And once in Paris, they could both eat an inordinate amount of boeuf bourguignon.

The manager said he didn't know how to break it to me but

felt that someone had to since it was a common confusion and he could sympathize.

Break what to me?

LaCroix isn't French, it comes from La Crosse, Wisconsin, and a brewery that used to make lagers.

Lagers?

Yeah, lagers.

But that's not even remotely French.

They're German, said the manager. Bavarian.

Can't be.

Afraid so.

Sans cans, I walked back to my building in a daze. The doorman was not at his desk either, and there was no sign of where he had gone or when he would be back. I had to let myself into the building with a key and push the elevator buttons myself.

Upstairs, I found my apartment transformed. A new dining table had been brought in, rectangular and long, with rows of appetizers, crackers, nuts, marinated olives, various-colored dips laid out down its spine, and more cubed cheese than I'd ever seen. This not-mine table ran from the edge of the kitchen to the other side of the living room, right up next to Suede Chair. People I didn't know were meandering around this table, picking at food. A nightmare? I closed my eyes and rubbed them. When I opened them again, the scene hadn't changed.

Joan! some elegantly dressed woman shouted from the bay window where she was drawing the blinds. We were going to surprise you but weren't sure when you would be back. Not everything is prepared yet and not everyone is here.

What's going on? I asked. Who are you?

Mark's idea, actually, said the man beside her, in a sweater vest and khakis, cradling a handful of nuts. Been planning it for days, told us all to keep it secret. The man pointed to my tallest book stalagmite and said I had some good ones in there, some of his faves. But he would be interested in my thoughts on them, and why I'd chosen to include certain titles over others, whenever I had a free minute to chat.

For the first time in a while, Mark was nowhere to be found.

My door opened, and in came the same weight and height couple from the elevator where they had been discussing apartment 9B and cultural moments. They handed me a bottle of wine and patted my shoulder. Nice to see you again, they said in unison, keep up the good work.

I took the bottle of wine and asked, What good work? But they had already moseyed on.

The door opened again and in came another stranger with another bottle of wine.

With no free hand left, I had to move away from the door and entryway. I backed myself into the kitchen and bumped into something. I turned, and the something was an Asian. Whoa, I said. I hadn't met other Asian tenants in the building before and assumed that I was the only one.

You lost? she asked, her lids dusted in a cool electric-blue shadow, her bangs cut on a slant. She introduced herself as the Korean exchange student subletting 4D for the year and studying graphic design at Columbia. Then she introduced herself as a postmillennial.

A what?

Because feeling lost is okay, she went on. I feel lost all the time.

For you, she said, and held out a packet of Chapagetti, or the best instant ramen that I would ever have. She handed me a round bowl of microwaveable rice and a tin of low-sodium Spam. The Spam should be fried and put over the rice in strips, like rays of a pink sun. If I felt adventurous, I could add a fried egg on top and blanched spinach on the side.

I brought my bottle-holding arms together and the cool, postmillennial Asian placed colorfully packaged food items into my embrace.

Let me know what you think about them, she said. Or don't. Whatever works. The Korean word for snacks is *gansik*, or "in-between foods," she told me, and without knowing why, except that there was something open about her, I told her that the Chinese word is *líng shí*, or "zero foods."

Friends, she stated, hooking her pinkie onto mine. She tugged and I wobbled, and would have dropped everything had Mark not appeared beside me right then and started taking the things out of my arms.

We have a wine rack, you know, he said.

We do? I said. Since when?

He'd brought one in last week.

Cute, said the postmillennial about us, and sauntered off to join the growing crowd in the living room. The door had been opening and closing intermittently. I took a peek and saw that there were close to ten people, huddled in two separate circles that were slowly merging.

I told Mark I couldn't go out there. I didn't know anyone, but somehow everyone seemed to know me. It was a trap.

They know you because I told them, he said.

What would possess you to do that? I asked.

Because this is your moment.

My kitchen counter held a dozen bottles now, and Mark was splitting them up into three groups by color. The sparkling and white he put in the fridge. The reds he started to uncork.

You used to be so busy with work, he said. But now that I was on leave or possibly suspended—which still pissed him off, by the way, and he kept mentioning that I should file a complaint about workplace abuse with HR—he thought I deserved a better, more welcoming experience and a chance to get to know the other tenants, as well as have them get to know me. They were all great people, cultured and easy to talk to. A woman who had recently been to Patagonia on a humanitarian trip to build houses. Another who teaches English to underserved communities. Even an art student from Korea, whom I'd just met and was experiencing her first dose of authentic American life. Mark had been meaning to get this group together for some time. He hoped to make introductions and to have us all connect. In case I wasn't up-to-date on lingo, he explained that these were like-minded folks, folks who were well informed, self-aware, or, as the kids say, woke.

I said I knew the word *woke*.

Oh, you do? He didn't think that I did.

Here I felt homesick. I missed my unit where every patient, however woke, was asleep.

Mark set out two champagne flutes. He went to the back of my fridge to pull out a bottle of what he considered the most appropriate celebratory champagne, Veuve Clicquot.

But what were we celebrating? That I was on leave for reasons that I myself couldn't keep straight, or that my apartment was no longer mine?

He poured the champagne out and the foam layers soared upward like rocket fuel. I held the flute by the stem with both hands to prevent myself from pulling out large quantities of my hair. He clinked his flute against mine, but it did not make a flute-like sound.

Cheers to the new Joan, he said, and reached for my elbow to escort me out into the living room, toward the crowd circle. New year, new Joan.

———

FOR SON OF A BITCH, you would say *wáng bā dàn,* or "turtle egg." Or character by character, taken quite literally, "king of eight eggs."

———

AFTER A BRIEF HELLO with everyone and hearing a sentence or two from them about what they did, I left the apartment at around 8:00 p.m., as the party was going on.

When the sweater vest man asked about my books again, I confessed to not having read any except the shortest. He thought I was joking, he laughed really hard. The elegantly dressed woman spoke about her extensive travels to South America. She told me that she'd been to China twice or thrice now. She loved visiting that country and asked which province my family was from. I said Jiangsu and she said she loved

Jiangsu, great food, a great balance of flavors in their dishes, the Jiangsu people were exceptionally skilled with steamed fish. Did I steam fish? I said no and she looked disappointed. The same weight and height couple were the English teachers. English was easy to learn but difficult to master, they told me, and while their students were earnest, the seemingly simple language was full of nuances that, after a certain point, became frustrating to explain. As native speakers, they weren't aware of the language's pitfalls until they saw their own students struggle with them. But what you're doing is so important, said the elegant woman to the couple, and all three of them beamed. Here the postmillennial graphic designer chimed in to say that to truly learn another language, you must listen to it through other mediums. She'd learned all her English from *Friends,* so English to her was mostly about cupping large mugs of coffee while expressing trivial but inconsistent thoughts. And you had to be funny in English, she said, or else it was a no go. The group nodded in unison. Everyone, even Mark, agreed that *Friends* was a good show.

When I left, I took only my work bag with wallet and phone and half an hour later was on the 8:46 p.m. Metro-North train to Greenwich. On board, I called my brother to say that I would be at the station shortly. He mentioned how late it was and last minute, but he commended me on having come to my senses, our previous conversation must have really sunk in. Negotiation 101: Everything is negotiable except for what is not—seeing your family on important dates, being there for them when they decide to host important events.

Almost too ironic that I was fleeing one crowd of people for another, trading a house party in for a bash. How did I get myself into this situation? Which tests of being an effective hermit had I failed?

I said yeah, well. I asked if Tami could lend me some clothes.

Everything all right? he asked.

Totally fine, I said.

At pickup, he was waiting for me in their new Land Rover. After I got in, he pointed out the car's leather-lined interior, the broad clamshell hood, the exterior color of Yulong white. This was their newest plug-in hybrid model. On a full battery, it could do about seventy-five miles of mixed city driving.

Mixed city driving is key, I said.

He drove us through the town center and said had it been earlier and light out, he could have at least shown me around. He didn't understand why I executed my personal plans without foresight or consideration for others. What if he hadn't picked up the phone, hadn't heard it? Then I would've had to find a way to their house on my own at night. Greenwich was safe, but no place is that safe after dark.

From downtown we drove past the town's hospital that was barely visible now and that Fang pointed out each time we passed.

You could work there, you know, he said as he had before. Doctors here demand some of the highest hourly rates in the state, thus the country. Great work-life balance.

I nodded. But the squat brick building eerily aglow on my left had always seemed too pristine to be a hospital. There was no sense of danger or chaos. No contradictory signs like this way to emergency, but this way to ambulatory care. Left for billing, right for accounts payable. Down for lower floors, up for basement.

As Fang drove up their driveway and pulled into their garage, he asked if I was in some kind of trouble.

No trouble, I said.

From the garage we started walking along a scenic, pebbled footpath toward the main house, which had been extensively decorated for the new year with long, embroidered banners, flanking a newly painted red door, and groups of colorful lanterns evenly spaced around the porch. The footpath veered past the main house and into the back lawn, where the guesthouse stood, decorated more modestly with one lantern. I'd been telling Fang about my work situation, that I'd accumulated so many vacation days it was encouraged I take them all at once, which was very nice of the hospital wasn't it, very thoughtful and kind. Fang listened but I couldn't get a read on him. I couldn't tell if he suspected that I'd been fired and had nowhere else to go. I did have nowhere else to go, but theoretically, I still had a job.

On the guesthouse porch, Fang said that I could stay here for now and we would figure the rest out tomorrow. It's after ten, he said. Best not to wake up everyone else.

Been a while, hasn't it? I said fakely. How was the trip and beautiful Mountain Time Colorado?

Fang handed me a set of keys, along with a tote bag of Tami's clothes. His face had pinched, and under the small porch light, I could only see lines and shadows. He told me to cut the act. He knew that I'd been coming to see our mother in secret while they weren't home.

She told you, didn't she?

Course not. But it wasn't terribly hard to figure out or anyway that unpredictable. Ma can keep a secret, but you've never been a good liar.

I opened my mouth to say something but closed it again when I realized that it was a lost cause.

Everyone processes grief differently, and what Ma says, different people need different kinds of support.

But Fang could draw a direct line from my having spent only two days in China not grieving to my situation now. I was alone, thus lonely. I had no partner or children to help me get through. Yet the thought of family scared me, which was why I avoided it. I had to check those feelings from now on, he said, and get over them. A family is safe harbor, so it was crucial to establish yourself within this harbor, and to establish that harbor within a place.

Did we wish to be seen as immigrants forever, he asked, or did we want to become settlers of a place? Settlers created settlements and the ten-mile-radius target in Greenwich was meant to be that.

My turn to say that it was late and to unlock the guesthouse door and go inside.

You've always been like this, he said, everything on your own terms, no regard for the big picture.

———

I HAD TROUBLE SLEEPING that night. Outside was too quiet, the guesthouse even more so, and Tami's nightgown was too long for me at the bottom, in the sleeves, was too perfumed around the neck.

Sleep, I said, and my brain said no.

A direct line? I could draw one from Fang having felt denied everything to denying himself nothing. From him having been left behind by our parents to his belief system now. Control, being close enough to control, following a plan.

His big-picture plan, long established, was that progress came in three waves. The first wave was our parents, who took any job available and occupied the lowest social rung. In their discontent, they invested in their children, us, and we would go on to rebuild the wealth that had been lost. The third wave, my brother's children, would be the first to benefit from a safety net created by wave two. Finally, they could take risks, pursue passions, and, as my brother believed, make us culturally ascendant. It was then three waves until fiscal and social success, and my big-picture job was to provide a third, which is the part that I had trouble with. If I never married or had children, it was heavily implied that all this planning was for naught.

Was it harder to be a woman? Or an immigrant? Or a Chinese person outside of China? And why did being a good any of the above require you to edit yourself down so you could become someone else?

As my brother liked to point out, the cycle was vicious and unending. The *Mayflower* carried the first Americans, but newcomers seen as too foreign are so often labeled "fresh off the boat." Immigrants become settlers who go on to call out the new immigrants. The *Mayflower* was centuries ago, I'd said, making excuses, I suppose, for the *Mayflower*. What about the railroads? he replied. The gold rush wasn't so long ago. Fang cared about U.S. history way more than I did and had sat me down before for lessons.

Following the gold rush, after the completion of the rail-roads, the Chinese accounted for 0.002 percent of the U.S. pop-ulation but were blamed for stealing American jobs. Entire communities were massacred, entire groups of Chinese men, women, kids. To solve the problem of job theft and thus the massacres, exclusion laws were enacted for the next sixty-some years. The women were banned first, as few were believed to have come to America for honorable work. Whores. Concu-bines. Hard not to wonder if the ban's more insidious motive was breeding—remove the women first, tarnished already, and you stem an unwanted population. After the men were banned, no Chinese were allowed into the country or allowed to return if they'd left. Chinatowns, Chinese food, the red gates of equality that sometimes led to dingy streets where the aliens, or so the leftover Chinese were known, could retreat. The first immigrants were barred from citizenship, owning property, and marrying outside of their race. A woman took the citizen-ship of her husband then, so equally unfortunate for the China-man who could not gain citizenship was the woman who, if born here, would lose hers for marrying him. And who would've married the long-suffering Chinaman then, except for the longer-suffering Chinawoman? By no coincidence, the year the ban was lifted was at the end of the Second World War, when China was our ally against Japan and a third of the Japanese population in America, mostly citizens, had already been interned. As a token of thanks, the Chinese were granted paths to citizenship, and for the next twenty years, the annual immigration quota for the Chinese was raised to a generous 105, a number that still worried some Americans who believed if you give those greedy aliens an inch, they will take a mile.

U.S. history was appalling, but I also didn't know what my brother expected me to do about it. These events predated us and our parents. We weren't descendants of railroad workers or the first Chinatown restaurateurs.

Nothing to do with us? he'd say. How many ethnic groups has this country ever banned? History repeats itself. Asians are often pitted against other Asians, and even citizenship can't always save you.

If history did repeat itself, then I needed only to wait for the next round to experience the trauma firsthand. Though maybe the next round was now in my exile from the hospital, the city, apartment 9A, and a virus problem on the other side of the world.

A daughter of immigrants is the daughter of guests, is a part-time guest herself, and the best kind of guest goes with the flow. She stays in a guesthouse.

Asians are often pitted against other Asians—when my brother broached the subject, I didn't give it another second of thought because medicine still strove to reward merit and the system had treated me well. But at every application gate and interview, I was not so subtly reminded that I wasn't competing against white or black Americans, I was competing against the Koreans, the Japanese, and other Chinese Americans vying for the exact same spot.

Quotas haven't gone away, nor have the large groups of us willing to race against time and one another, but never call ourselves a race.

Proud to be an American, a feeling that I lacked but also a phrase that I didn't think applied to me.

So, *othering,* did that term apply to me and was it what I'd internalized? Whenever I heard news of deportation or the line that people must enter the legal way, fear of my own removal would start to reflux. Then I had to remind myself that I was born here, that this land was as much mine as it was theirs. But were these facts written on my face? Was my being born here and my parents' legal arrival carved into our facial features or the color of our skin? And even if I hadn't been born here, had I been one of those kids brought over by her parents at age two, five, twelve, then naturalized, what made them and their families any less American if they were the most American of all things—fresh off the boat, in search of better days?

Little you can do about which era or group you're set into here, was another direct line that I could draw. An immigrant family controls nothing, and so raises two average children obsessed with gaining it back, albeit in different ways. The same trait that I was criticizing Fang for was what I liked about attending intensive care units. A ring of twenty beds, an entire wing of the hospital, all under my domain.

———

SLEEP NEVER CAME, SO I just lay there for hours, watching light come in through the window, through the blinds. I looked for cracks in the ceiling (none found). I started to hear not street noise, as in New York, but small, faint sounds—the breeze of a passing car, maybe that cab and its driver.

Then I got up and washed my face.

The kitchen windows were fogged, and as I was wiping off the condensation, I could vaguely make out two figures coming down the footpath from the main house under a giant black umbrella. When the aide and my mother came inside, they dusted off their thick coats and collapsed the umbrella with the push of a button. My mother was holding a small pot; the aide, a tray of tiny dishes.

Nanny's congee, my mother said, lifting the small pot and nudging the aide, who said she was only following my mother's instructions.

But improved upon, my mother said.

Alongside rice porridge, they had brought me pickled vegetables, a fermented tofu cube, Jif creamy peanut butter, a hunk of which I plopped right at the edge of my bowl such that it moved down into the congee like a mudslide. Buns filled with sweet custard, buns filled with red bean, savory buns with spinach and minced meat, sticky rice and pork belly wrapped in bamboo leaves and tied with string.

You made *zòng zi*? I asked, the entire breakfast table covered in food.

I had to, she said. Yesterday, I was so bored, and this was the most time-consuming thing I could think of to do. My own grandmother's recipe, your great-grandmother, who sadly you've never met. But what a good daughter you are, she added with sarcasm, to not even tell me that you were coming, to just show up.

Not very filial, I said.

No, she said.

I felt something in my eyes. A tear or dried specks of dust? I hadn't cried at my father's funeral and saw very few people who did. My mother's eyes were red during the service, but she had cried elsewhere, alone and out of sight. There was sadness in the room, a large rolling cloud of it, but also the expectation to not let your own show.

Triggered by as simple an act as my mother bringing me food and ordering me to eat.

Triggered by as simple a scene as a random father pushing the backs of two young kids across the street, pushing them to school and their futures, I have been on the verge of tears before. The welling up inside me, enormous amounts of water, and then forcing the water back down.

Much of any culture can be linked back to eating and food, food and care, eating and language. To eat one's feelings, to eat dust, words, to eat your own heart out, to eat someone else alive, to eat your cake and have it too, things that are adorable (puppies, babies) that are said to be good enough to eat, to have someone else eat out of the palm of your hand, to be chewed out, a dog-eat-dog world. Chinese isn't any different from English in this way. *Chī* for "eat," and *chī sù,* to only eat vegetables but also, colloquially, to be a pushover. *Chī cù,* to eat vinegar or be jealous. *Chī lì,* to eat effort, as for a task that is very strenuous. To eat surprise, to be amazed, *chī jīng*. To be completely full or *chī bǎo fàn,* and thus to have nothing better to do. To eat punishment or get the worst of it, *chī kuī*. And, most important, to eat hardship, suffering, and pain, *chī kǔ,* a defining Chinese quality, to be able to bear a great deal without showing a crack.

The price of success is steep and I've never been able to distinguish it from the feeling of sacrifice. If I could hold success in my hand, it would be a beating heart.

—

ON FEBRUARY 1, THERE were more than fourteen thousand cases of the virus in China and more than three hundred deaths. All forty-two Apple stores in China had closed (following the closures of both Starbucks and Ikea), out of what the CEO stated to be an abundance of caution, and with twelve cases confirmed, Australia would deny entry to all foreign nationals traveling from China. No deaths outside of the mainland, eight cases in the United States, which had announced its own ban on Chinese travelers the day before.

On February 1, the New Year bash was happening, as planned, over in the main house. While the caterers were still setting up, I'd gone inside to fix myself a plate of food and say hello to my nephews. This three-person blob was always moving, sprinting, and play-fighting with one another with plastic guns that shot foam bullets. I asked the blob how school was going, and since no one wanted to talk about that, our interactions stopped there.

You could be a good aunt, Tami would often remind me in the same breath as pointing out which thing around me I'd treated as my surrogate child.

That I didn't like kids was her suspicion, and that I'd remained childless not by choice but from some horrible mental or biological glitch. I didn't dislike kids, I'd said, and I certainly didn't dislike my nephews. But you're not in love with them, you don't coo after them, she'd explained. When they were small, you never asked to hold them, which had hurt her, my not wanting to hold my own nephews and cradle them or put them on my shoulder and fly them around like human planes. (I feared that I would drop them. I had no natural desire to hold a child.) And why is that? A woman's maternal instincts are strong and the smell of a baby's head is like freshly baked bread. (I had none of these instincts, it seemed. I couldn't smell the bread.)

When I found Fang in the foyer, supervising a small crew as they hung up festive decor, I told him that I wasn't planning to stay at the party.

He didn't look up from his phone and was rapidly tapping away on its screen.

You're mad at me, I said.

And you're difficult, he said.

But so are you.

He glanced up for a second, one eyebrow cocked, and I knew what he wanted to say—yeah, but not as difficult as you, no one is as difficult as you—and had he said that, I would have taken the bait, I would have escalated it—except that would have made us children, two brats, aka siblings, bickering about who was more of a pain in the ass, more spoiled, and who our parents liked more.

Suit yourself, he said.

So, since I wasn't at the party, I could only hear the music and sounds of guests arriving, greetings of joy. I could watch from the guesthouse windows their cars, a string of them, being parked along the driveway by a courteous valet. Then around 10:00 p.m. or so, as I was watching TV and giving myself half an hour more before bed, my mother came into the guesthouse and plopped beside me on the couch. She asked to stay in the second bedroom for the night. The main house was too loud. For activities, Fang had hired an ice sculptor and a pianist. The sculptor was a small Asian man who carried a foot-long electric sword and hacked away at ice blocks for hours to turn them into ice animals, like prosperous fish and rats. The pianist was a tall Asian woman who sat in the foyer, in front of a white baby grand, pounding away at it with dramatic chords.

And then there was the dragon, my mother said.

Dragon?

The one that had been hung up on the foyer ceiling and wound its way through the rooms and into the kitchen. Thirty feet long from head to tail, and made from papier-mâché.

Oh, that dragon, I said.

We continued to watch TV, and she asked what show it was that we had been watching.

A sitcom called *Friends,* I said, about six friends who lived in Manhattan with entry-level jobs but palatial apartments, and about chatting in English with coffee mugs.

*Friends,* my mother said, but after one commercial break started calling it, in English, *Buddies*.

Kind of silly to watch. *Buddies*. I don't like the constant laugh track. I don't get any of their jokes.

———

THE NAMES MY PARENTS had given themselves were Jim and Sue. Ill fitting but easy, though sometimes even they forgot to respond to them. Jim? No Jim here. Oh sorry, you mean me.

The name they had given me was *Jiu-an,* the simplest Chinese equivalent to *Joan*. I knew of another Asian Joan in the hospital, many Jessicas, Emilys, and Lindas. Only Asians outside of Asia chose names for themselves that took into account the convenience of others or smoothed out their foreign names to be less offensive to the ear. Like my parents, Tami had found her name in a book, a few months before she was set to arrive. *Fang* is not pronounced like the very sharp tooth, as he told people that it was, but closer to *fong,* although not quite like *fong*.

Each Chinese sound has four tones, and within each tone of a sound there are many characters. The strokes of the characters matter for balance, symmetry. It's meant to be art.

*Jiù* (就), fourth tone, twelve strokes, means "at once" or "right away" or "moving toward." *Ān* (安), first tone, six strokes, is "peace," or, taken apart, it's a roof (宀) under which there is a woman (女). What this woman does, no one really knows. She might be happy or sad. She might be hardworking or indolent, but put this woman in a house and you will have serenity and ease. *Jiu-an* (就安), or just peace or simply a woman in a house.

—

BY FEBRUARY 5, THE number of cases in China had doubled to twenty-eight thousand. A flight from Korea originally set to land in Las Vegas was diverted to LAX, when the crew was notified that three passengers on board, three U.S. citizens, had been to China in the past fourteen days. The crew must have then alerted the passengers, and all two hundred passengers must have glanced at the most Chinese-seeming face nearby and wondered, Was it you? Could you possibly, probably, be one of the disease carriers forcing us to land in a completely different state?

I couldn't help but recall the airline receptionist at Pudong who already thought I had some disease, when that was still just a joke, from one Chinese person to another.

My mother now visited me in the guesthouse every afternoon. She would bring me clothes, brown turtleneck and vest combos, wool socks, that fit better than Tami's but made me look like my mother. Sometimes we matched totally and the aide would say that we looked like a couple. That's scary, I said and my mother said we all become our mothers, it's inescapable, but what's so scary about coupling with me, for forty long weeks, you lived inside me and you and I were one. I had no good response to that, so we put the kettle on, made tea, and watched any television except international news. Instead of sitting with us on the sofa, the aide would move in and between the rooms, trying to find something to tidy. I told her there was nothing to tidy, I'd been cognizant of not making a mess. But the aide was determined, and often after they left, I would find in the bathroom the first square of the toilet paper roll folded into such an intricate design that it was almost too pretty to be used.

February 8 was the fifteenth day of the first lunar month, or *yuán xiāo. Yuán,* "first," and *xiāo,* "night," is a holiday to admire paper lanterns and eat round sweet dumplings with friends and family. The rounded shape represents *tuán jié,* or "unity."

My mother and the aide had made some and brought them over to the guesthouse. While the three of us ate, my mother announced that she'd booked the first available plane ticket back to Shanghai in mid-March, with Air China, which would never be one of the airlines to ban China, since the crew and company were Chinese. Mid-March was the earliest time she could find. All of February had been booked up.

I pushed the rice spheres around in their soup.

She told me to stop playing with my food.

My mother and her siblings were on a group chat, and more often than before, I would see her scroll through her phone to check if anyone over there was up. The official word from Air China was that by March, its normal flight itinerary would resume.

One sister who was a nurse told my mother not to fret. March was a full month away. The infected cities had been sealed off, new hospitals were being built overnight, and unless you were essential personnel, no one was allowed to leave their house. Such rules were being enforced, you could be fined or arrested for being out without notice. You couldn't even go to the bank without an official approval slip and someone coming to your door in a hazmat suit for a temperature check.

Their brother was the silent type, but he sent a daily ticker of total case counts and deaths.

Why had none of the siblings emigrated? I imagined not because they doubted the opportunities abroad but because there was no impetus to leave. When my parents returned to China, their families folded them naturally back in. When asked about their time in America, they framed it as neither a total failure or success.

Then there were some immigrants who had no desire to go back. Tami would leave the place of her birth with no intention to return. In my brother's big-picture plan, I didn't know which wave she was, the first or the second. Given that her parents had stayed behind, she technically belonged to the first, but she faced less resistance than my parents, her accent wasn't an impediment, and material success had come quick. Tami left China in her early twenties, at least a decade earlier than my parents, who often complained of coming over too late and having to *pīn mìng,* or "fight for life" to catch up. Had they just left even five years earlier, their minds more malleable, bodies energized, they might have caught up and stayed.

How immigration is often described: a death, a rebirth. Or how my mother would describe it, starting back down at zero. To *pīn* can also mean to piece together, as you would a puzzle. So, to piece back together life.

I'd known that for years Tami had been trying to move her parents from Chongqing to Greenwich. I wasn't in the main house to hear the call she'd apparently just had with them, but as my mother told it, Tami was saying that now might be the time to act, should borders truly close—if that were to happen indefinitely, when or how would families split overseas be able to see each other again?

As my mother was talking, details about Tami came back to me. During her master's, she had gone, as did most international Chinese students, the entire two-year stint without flying back to see her family (doctorates went longer, sometimes five, six, nine years). The primary reason being cost, she couldn't afford the round-trip airfare on the stipend. But even if she'd been able to, I doubt she would've gone. None of these international students wished to give the school that had sponsored them the impression that they were taking unnecessary time off.

Grad school burned Tami out. Or it was the years of schooling beforehand and maybe the fatigue of having been sent down a conveyor belt of achievement tasks to be exported as a commodity. Her parents had other plans for her, that after the master's, she would continue on to the doctorate, then after the doctorate, import herself back to China to find that high-paying academic job. There was no doctorate but there was a wedding. And so quick after marrying my brother did she become the sister-in-law who shook her bejeweled wrist of status at me that I'd almost forgotten about the Tami who had arrived here status-less, on a student visa, and knew no one except an advisor and a school liaison who picked her up from JFK.

Tami's parents remained unhappy with the outcome. They came for the wedding, and after the birth of each grandson, but stayed no more than a week. I knew that they'd made some blunt remarks to Tami. I knew they'd said, Why did you go to America just to be a mom? You could have done that in China, without all those years of education and the distance. Remembering this again, I saw Tami's pursuit of motherhood in a new light. The critique was harsh, but for parents like those, much had been at stake, substantial sacrifice and pulling out of the heart. A daughter lost, in a way, to another place, and had they had a do-over, they might not have encouraged her to leave. Tami's parents refused to move to America and have never wavered on that decision. A permanent move overseas at their age would be crippling. If they couldn't read, write, or speak the language, then they regressed, relying heavily on Tami for everything that in China they could do on their own. China was their home, and there, they had good pensions, a spacious apartment, independence. The same things that my mother had there and wanted back. So why move to the land of the free to not be? Whatever mile radius Tami had envisioned for them was not what they wanted for themselves.

But don't you want to be near your grandkids? she'd said on the call, many calls.

I can't help you from here. I can't always get there in time.

And what if something happens to one of you? What then?

Yes, what if something did happen, like sudden death, a freak accident, like tripping over projector cords and hitting your head.

The last detail about my sister-in-law that occurred to me was that because of the one-child policy, she was their only one. She had no siblings back in China to help care for her parents as my parents had theirs, as I had Fang to look after our mother here. Hence, if she could not go to them, and they would not come to her, then what becomes of their family, the first that Tami had known?

That family becomes amputated, as do the people within them. Limbs feel hacked off, and you find yourself hobbling around on one leg. Or how I felt after my parents emigrated back when I was still in college, and how I felt about my family in China, who had carried on long enough without me and I had lost the opportunity to know.

———

THOUGH IT SEEMED THAT I didn't know my family here any better.

Mornings I spent in the main house, with breakfast set at 7:00 a.m. as Tami and the housekeeper tried to get three boys ready for school. Neat uniforms. Clean shoes. Black hair combed to the side with a wet comb or just the palm of their mother's hand. String cheese, orange juice, buttered bread, all laid out on the kitchen island for the boys to stop and grab like race cars. I would exchange a few words with my brother, who was always on his phone checking end-of-day numbers from the Asia markets, while waiting for the company chauffeur to come pick him up. How had I slept? More coffee? Tea? Biscuit? That each morning there was always a plate of warm biscuits on the counter astounded me. It was all the comforts of a home that no adult here had grown up with but now had. The aide would arrive—hello, waves—and set down her things before going upstairs to fetch my mother, who had been allowing herself to sleep in. Three book bags were brought out, strapped on, after which my brother went over to give each son a head pat, the youngest a pick-up hug, and then Tami ushered all of them out the door. Quiet for a moment, before I heard the sounds of Tami pulling out of the garage and speeding down the driveway, since they were already late, then not long after, the sounds of a slick black sedan slowly pulling up. If done with his coffee, Fang would leave. If our mother had come down by then, he would peck her on the cheek.

I was confused and made more confused by scenes of physical affection I'd never seen. I wondered why I'd never seen it or if I'd never looked. No, I had looked before when it'd been just Fang, me, and our parents, and physical affection was hard to find. Like night and day, comparing this breakfast scene with those of my youth, when sometimes no parent was around and the only noise was the clinking of my spoon against my cereal bowl, a dim flush mount overhead.

By Valentine's Day, the case number in China had doubled again, to just over sixty-six thousand. In a speech to the nation,

Xi Jinping called the disease a big test for the country, but that they would all, all 1.4 billion Chinese people, cross the river in the same boat, or so the idiom went. Fifteen cases in the United States, when the CDC announced that the disease still had a lot of unknowns and some screening kits had been found to be faulty.

On Valentine's Day, Fang and Tami went out to eat, just the two of them, leaving my mother and me to watch the boys. We ordered pizza.

When both Fang and Tami ate with us, so much dinner talk revolved around my nephews and their activities. The youngest had started to play tennis, which the middle and oldest sons already played. Fang added a fourth, and now there was serious hope for a doubles match sometime down the line. Boys needed tennis, my brother still said, otherwise they won't turn out right. Fang wasn't a strict dad, but he spoke to each son in turn and like small adults. Name three things you did today; list the three you plan on doing tomorrow. He had a 60-40 rule, that 60 percent of his parent voice should be used in praise, 40 percent in constructive criticism. Tami had no such ratio and was far less strict. After dinner, she instituted game night or put on a movie. She would tell the boys to shower, brush their teeth, go to bed, but then be lulled into another ten-minute extension. Was she trying to be a better mother than hers had been to her? Than mine had been to us? A fun mom, or the most American of all things, a mom who was also a friend. Circumstances improve. Time, money, the question of survival no longer hanging overhead. As a child, I hadn't felt my situation to be lacking until I became an adult. Because a child can get used to anything, a child will find a way to grow up.

After the entire Valentine's pizza was consumed, I heard myself say the same thing to my nephews. Shower, brush your teeth, go to bed.

But it's only seven p.m., they replied.

Then just shower.

What about a story or game night or a movie?

I said I couldn't be like their mother.

What about homework?

It's not done?

We're done with homework.

So, it is done.

Not what we said.

Took me another second to realize that by "done with homework" they meant they were over it and unable to get back into it. Harder to watch my nephews do no work for the evening than to take all of their pages and finish it myself. Paperwork could be glorious, and I hadn't filled out any since going on leave.

You might have been tricked, said my mother, who found me at the edge of the dining table with a stack of worksheets and a calculator, trying to write my numbers like a child.

Shower, brush your teeth, go to bed, I told her as well.

—

RECENTLY, I'VE NOTICED SOMETHING. I looked down at my hands and noticed that they are the same shape as my father's.

The same square fingers and fingernails, the same knuckle protrusions and creases around the joints. Not possible, of course, especially with the creases, but once I noticed, I couldn't stop staring at them. I couldn't stop holding my hands out and inspecting them from different angles, then looking at myself in a mirror. My face, stature, and the sharp drop of my shoulders were my mother's. But how I held a fork, chopsticks; how my hands gestured, flexed, and sat in my lap, fingers naturally curled in.

The only difference was that his hands were perpetually pruned and cracked. The smell of grease would radiate off his skin the moment he entered a room. Dandruff on his shoulders, a heavy dusting of it in his hair from dry scalp, but that looked like fine, crumbled plaster. His shoes smelled bad; his feet could smell worse. For half an hour after work he would have to stand in the shower. Outside, in the kitchen, my mother, nose pinched, holding his stained work shirt by the smallest amount of fabric, between her index finger and thumb, and with her arm outstretched, sprinting to the sink as fast as possible where it would be soaked. He was not unclean, yet I thought this, me, his own daughter. He was not withdrawn, unfeeling, incompetent, bumbling, a fish out of water, yet I've thought all those things as well. I was guilty of having the impressions of him that a stranger might at first glance. But as his daughter, I should have tried harder, while I still had the chance, to draw him out, to listen and to champion him, them both.

My mother's hands weren't so much pruned as sanded down from years of cleaning products and bleach. Her palm lines shallow etches, her fingerprints gone.

They must have fought a ton, but I was buffered from it. Before Fang arrived, I was too young to understand, and after he was here, he could listen on my behalf. The moment he noticed something was off, that a serious fight was about to start, he would say in Chinese, Hey, Jiu-an, let's go outside.

But it's freezing out, I replied in English, since there's no greater way to hurt your family than to not speak in their native tongue even when you can.

So? You chicken? (His English fast improving.) Come on, little chicken, let's go.

Dozens of times he called me "little chicken" and took me outside to play. When we came back an hour later, the fight was over.

I had taught my father the meaning of that phrase, fish out of water, but he was the one who had taught me. So, here you say "fish out of water." But there, you would say "like a fish to water," or *rú yú dé shuǐ* (如鱼得水)—like a stranded fish put back. He rested his case again. East and west will never get along, never see eye to eye.

Did he mean us? Was he the east and I the west, two fish arguing about the idioms to which they belonged?

Other questions I'd never asked my parents, never thought to find out: Did they fight less after they returned to China? My father soon found better work, and they bought their apartment that was on a high floor and had a closed-in balcony. That their standard of living improved so quickly made me wonder once why they didn't move back sooner, say ten or fifteen years earlier, why stay so long in America, for what, for whom—proof that even smart people can ask dumb questions. And if they weren't fighting as much, what were they doing in their less stressed-out spare time? I couldn't imagine my parents with leisure, with fun (or knowing what to do with leisure if our most prized trait was to endure), but that's my blind spot, not theirs. For I knew that they did have fun, through the occasional photo sent over, shots of just the two of them standing side by side next to a turtle pond, or group shots of them at yet another banquet table with unfamiliar faces. Who's that? I would ask, and get, Old classmates, old friends. We all went out singing last week, or dancing, or turtle watching.

---

ON PRESIDENTS' DAY I texted Madeline to wish her a happy Presidents' Day, since I knew she had the Monday off. She texted back that it was snowing, and whenever she looked outside her window, she felt like she was living in a snow globe, which was nice. She was home all day with her boyfriend and their plants, binge-watching *West Wing*. I said how appropriate. A common question we asked patients coming out of sedation, to test their cognition, was who the current president was. Sometimes they gave fictional names like Jed Bartlet, and she finally wanted to know who that was. Now she was deep into season four.

Reese had returned from his wellness retreat and was back on service, she wrote.

I wrote that I was jealous. How long was he on?

Two straight weeks, half of them nights.

The director was clearly punishing Reese, but I could feel my face heat up. It seemed unfair to put Reese on that schedule, while letting me rest idle and eat steak tartare. (A dish the chef had prepared the other night, that while delicious, I couldn't get through without imagining the red mound as my brain and here was my silver spoon of relaxation, of privilege, scooping away my brain content, leaving me bare. My mother didn't touch hers. She had gotten into one of her honest moods and was questioning the way Fang did things like why would you serve me cold and uncooked meat with a raw egg? A proper part of fine dining, he said. And, he thought, something new that they could all try. You don't have to eat it, Ma, we can get you soup. But why did we need fine dining in the home? she asked. What was wrong with regular, everyday dining?)

Over text, Madeline made fun of Reese some more: supposedly he had a new girlfriend and had almost cleaned off his desk.

Then she started typing something. The ellipse bubble appeared, disappeared, appeared again. The text that finally came through wasn't long but it was serious. She said she didn't want to cause undue panic and nothing official had been announced, but the hospital had been preparing and directors were meeting behind closed doors. Cases in Europe were on the rise. Two weeks, she predicted, bed capacity would have to double, all specialties redeployed, and all off-service attendings called back.

I said I could already see it coming.

What? she wrote. The shitstorm?

At least China's curve had started to bend.

China's China, said Madeline. But what about Western countries, those with more liberties, diversity, and an entrenched sense of the self? Her family in Germany kept asking her if they should be worried. The first case had arrived in Bavaria, where her mother and sister still lived.

And what did you say? I asked.

I said you should be worried, she said. She advised her mother to stop leaving the house, which her mother refused to do, since this mother came from strong stock and parents who had lived through the war, so what was a small virus compared to the Nazi army marching through her hometown. Her other response to Madeline's warning was to ask her daughter if living in America for so long had melted her core. Germans did not know fear, they could take anything on (in other words, Germans could eat pain too). So no, Madeline's mother was not going to stop leaving the house every day for fresh bread, though she appreciated her Americanized daughter's concern.

Stubborn mothers, difficult ones.

Sorry, I wrote, with a sad face.

What can you do? Madeline replied, with Blonde Shrugging Woman emoji.

Before she went back to *West Wing,* I told her what I'd learned about LaCroix and its hidden Bavarian past. That's scandalous, she said. Turning lager into calorie-free sparkling water.

———

ON FEBRUARY 20, HUBEI Province reported just 349 new cases, the epicenter's lowest daily count since the start. An American couple was taking a six-month-long cruise around the world, when in Japan, the husband's temperature spiked and he had to be taken off the ship and isolated at a local hospital. Now the wife was back in the U.S. while the husband was still in Japan. The husband told CNN that being apart and stranded gave him a strange feeling of loneliness—you're all by yourself, and there's nobody else here to take care of you (except for the Japanese nurses and doctors). He wished to be reunited with his wife and believed that the best care he could get was on his own home soil.

Home soil.

Home plate.

But what does the soil of home feel like? Because doesn't all soil, at some point, get stuck under your nails and need to be cleaned out?

My mother and Fang argued more openly now. She would say what was another virus compared to what she'd handled in her adult life. She was tough.

Mentally tough did not equal physically tough, Fang would explain, and should she really get sick, determination to get well did not change the quality of her immune system or turn back time. You're seventy, Ma.

She said she was sixty-nine. Her birthday was in November and she refused to turn seventy in this country, she simply refused to be here that long.

Fang tried to loop me into it, but I couldn't do it. I couldn't take sides. Even though my brother was right.

I just don't understand, Tami would say. Are you uncomfortable here? Have we made you feel unwelcome? Do you need more space?

When Air China postponed my mother's March flight, then a day later canceled it, she came to the guesthouse to vent again and to call the airline's customer service so she could vent to the first available agent.

Yes, hi, hello, I have some thoughts about what you're trying to do to us. I left to visit my children as any newly widowed mother might for what I believed would just be a few months, and now you won't let me back in, your own nationals. You're trying to strand us and keep us in some kind of limbo. We're expendable to you.

The agent apologized for any inconvenience, but there was really nothing he could do, these were government mandates, which flights were cleared for entry and which were not. Temporary measures, meant to reduce traffic and funnel international travelers through select airports that were able to handle individual screening.

How am I an international traveler? she asked. I live there. I was born there. I'm a citizen. Also, the daily case count was falling, so why was travel getting more restricted instead of relaxing?

The agent mentioned cases elsewhere.

But those are still so low. Why are you doing this to me? What kind of customer service is this?

Free of charge, the agent offered to put her on the next available flight in April, which is when they hoped to resume their normal flying schedule. He thanked her for her patience.

———

TWICE A WEEK, AN American grocery van came to my brother's house to deliver freshness and variety, then a second van would come carrying only Chinese produce and snacks. My mother shelled sunflower seeds at a rate of half a bag an hour. She preferred only specific brands of dried prunes and steamed sponge cakes only from Chinese bakeries. The drivers would unload their respective vans. The housekeeper and aide would stock the fridge and pantry. When my mother asked to help, she would be told that all the heavy lifting had been done.

But why is brown bread in America more expensive than white? she asked, peering into bags of insulated foil from the first van. Why is brown rice here more expensive than white? In China, it's just the reverse. Because white rice takes longer to process and should cost more.

In China, public schools are better than private ones.

In China, students do their own homework because students are assiduous.

Said to me, as I was hunched over a new stack of paperwork, courtesy of my nephews.

I said I enjoyed it.

You enjoy doing other people's work for them? she asked.

I said sort of, it made me feel needed or whatever.

But then the other person doesn't learn, she said. You're hurting the other person by taking away their chance to suffer.

In China, everyone knows how to suffer because everyone is assiduous.

In China, he and I were considered urbanites and well positioned to immigrate.

In China, I didn't think immigrating would be so hard, I didn't think it would be like this.

You're not immigrating again, Mom, I had to remind her. You're just here for a long visit.

Oh, she would say, snapping out of her trance and noticing

that I was still sitting beside her. She must have been recalling a time before me, and when she and my father were still young. The date of her newly scheduled April flight would miss Qing-ming Jie, or Tomb-Sweeping Day. Who would clean off her husband's tomb and place fresh flowers on the mantel? She could ask one of her sisters to do it, but it wouldn't be the same. The first year he was gone, and she wouldn't be there to pay her respects. She talked to him before bed now, as if he were in the room, about to go to sleep. She told him about her boring days.

Then her mood shifted. A glint of an idea had formed, caus-ing her to tap the kitchen counter excitedly. What if we drove to the airport right now and spoke to an Air China employee in person? Once they heard her story, they would have to put her on a plane.

I said I wasn't driving her to the airport.

What if she drove herself?

You can't drive here, Mom. The green card is not a license, etc.

But what if I did?

What if you drove? What if you got on the highway?

I could, you know. I'm your mother. I've crossed more bridges than you have.

That's a metaphor. Those are figurative bridges.

She grimaced and looked away. When she looked back at me, it was clear she was angry. How right you are, Joan-na. Everything about you is so perfect and right. Lucky me to have a daughter like you. She stared daggers into me and I knew this to be a challenge.

I held my hands out and asked what she wanted me to do.

Nothing, she said. You don't need to do anything since you're already the perfect daughter.

I told her to stop calling me that.

Then stop treating me like a child.

When she looked away again, I wondered if this was what she was thinking but didn't know how to express: In China, I might be a widow, but at least I'm not a child. Just because I've lost my husband doesn't mean I've lost my mind, and what I need help with isn't money or food, but something else entirely.

I said I would let her drive down the driveway and back up, but only if I sat in the passenger seat, with my hand on the emergency brake.

What about Nanny?

She can sit in the back.

My mother chose Fang's new Land Rover, clamshell white with red leather interiors and automatic closing doors. The driveway took a full minute to get down at ten miles an hour, with the sunroof lifted for the breeze. It was 34°F out, said the dashboard, and my mother had tied a scarf around her neck and turned on the radio to the first channel with music. Inevitably, I thought of the green Mustang, of Wendy's Frostys and of summer. Our nomadic family of four had spent only six summers together before Fang was off to college. There could never have been a childhood home, but after I went to college, there was no physical home at all.

Could one of your worries be that your family may have failed? a counselor once asked me.

Failed at what?

At being together, at placing a higher value on success than on keeping your unit together.

An odd question, I thought then, but an insular and short-sighted one, I think now. Some bonds are so forged in fire, some experiences are so permeated with feeling, that it is impossible to not see them with love.

At the end of the driveway, we checked the mailbox. Then my mother did a perfect U-turn and drove us back to the main house.

———

SINCE LEAVING THE CITY, I hadn't texted my cohost/neighbor about anything until he finally texted me.

Was I okay?

I am, I wrote. Was my apartment okay? The dining table taken out, all the extra chairs, everyone gone, the door locked and secure?

It is, he replied. And are the two of us okay? he asked. As neighbors and hopefully still friends, he hadn't meant to overstep.

But you did, I said.

Not his intention, and he was sorry.

I said I appreciated the apology.

Then he asked why I hadn't told him earlier that he was coming over too much and becoming a bother.

I would've stopped, he offered. Or at least toned it down. He'd assumed that I'd wanted him there, that I'd wanted the housewarming, I'd never mentioned otherwise.

Was never agreeing to something agreement? I wondered.

We should have communicated better, he said, and was upset at himself that we hadn't. What do you think? he asked. He felt that he'd always been clear about his intentions but maybe aspects were lost. Could we try from now on to say what we mean? He saw this as a chance for growth.

The lobe of rage burst in my head like a polyp. I could feel a liquid temper seeping out of my pores.

My epiphany. Mark was just like Reese—well-meaning in some ways, clueless in others. Neither could imagine having wasted another person's time or consuming every square inch of air in a room. Because Room People were full of themselves. They believed their own perspectives reigned supreme. And whereas I was taught to not stick out or aggravate your surroundings, to not cause any trouble and to be a good guest, someone like Mark was brought up with different rules—yes, push back, provoke, assert yourself, some trouble is good, since the rest of us will always go easy on you and, if anything, reward you for just being you. Not all of this was on him though. I shouldn't have opened my door to him and accepted his gifts. The spare key was a mistake, and my fault for not having spoken up sooner. That I'd believed everything he had to offer was valuable. My fault. A hundred percent accurate that I had no knowledge of the books he liked, baseball, television shows, charcuterie, and home decor. My uncouth assumption that when the French spoke about eating bread and pain, they were speaking to something that I knew very well. But not being steeped in the same culture as he was did not make me someone who needed his help, and that he'd acted like it was his job to improve me was both presumptuous and wrong. Why did he never consider the vice versa? For all his worldly and conscientious thoughts, wasn't I at least a person of two languages and two cultures? And to get to where I was today, didn't I know a few things he didn't?

I chose to not text him back or do what I wanted to do, which was call and lay into him until he could finally see where I was coming from. Expending more energy on him wasn't the answer. Why try to explain yourself to someone who had no capacity to listen?

—

MY HAIR HAD GROWN long and stringy. I washed it every other day but I rarely brushed it, and since there was no need to keep it out of my face anymore, I left it down. One weekend morning, early before anyone else was up, Tami in a beige sweater jogger set found me in my brown turtleneck. I'd been browsing coffee table books in their living room when, passing me from behind, she lifted a strand of my hair by its end and we both watched it listlessly fall. Then she sat down across from me and offered to take me to her salon so I could get that limp mess trimmed, blown dry, and tousled with a nutrient-rich mousse.

I said I didn't want my hair to look like a bird's nest.

Why would it look like a bird's nest? Does my hair look like that? No, so why would yours? I'm sitting here trying to help you. It was just a suggestion.

And like that we were arguing. From the sorry state of my hair to when I would be getting married and having my first child. He doesn't have to have means, she said about this elusive husband. Or a title, she added. As long as he was good to me. I let out a laugh and got back a glare. Tami asked why wasn't I more worried about these practical matters when people who never marry become outcasts, and a woman isn't a real woman until she's had a child.

Some words will take years to forgive. Or never. I, the childless non-woman and wife to zero senators, wished to reach out to my sister-in-law, but she also knew how to push me away. Has she forgiven her own parents for their dismay in her just becoming a mom? Hurt can be paid forward and often is, to make your own feel less.

Tami, these are my choices, not yours, I said. How you would handle a situation is not always mine.

Her head shrank a little back into her neck, and yet even so, she didn't develop a double chin or look any less refined.

What she was trying to say, she clarified, was that to grow, a woman must be willing to take on many roles. You can do anything well, Joannie, so I have no doubt that if you set your mind to being a wife and mother, you'll be fine, maybe even fantastic. Don't force yourself to be alone. Feminists have kids too.

I had many thoughts at that moment but no good reply. So, I just let my turn to speak run out until Tami started to talk again.

And once you have kids, no one will harangue you, not us, not anyone. No one will see you as a child anymore or assume that you've deviated from the path or missed out. As a mother, you become legitimate, thus untouchable. Consider it an out.

Of motherhood Tami had once said that there was no other job and I'd replied of course there were other jobs. Funny to me now how motherhood could work. That having a child made you a real woman who was no longer a child, but then once your own children became adults, you reverted back to the child.

Sounds of bare feet down the stairs, of hushed talking, and of my nephews trying to be discreet but failing. The fridge door opened but did not close.

I asked Tami how having kids was considered an out. The more I had, the more I would have to do, the more places I would have to go. Pediatrician visits alone, the dentist, emergency room scares, then back to the grocery store to stock up on more food. My mother would need to see them. From China she would fly over, and then my many kids and I would have to fly over there to see her.

Your mother is going to be here.

I said I didn't think so.

Tami's cheeks flushed and so had mine.

Can I ask you something? she said, her voice like a blade, and without waiting for my reply, asked, Do you see yourself as better than the nonworking woman? Is motherhood somehow beneath you?

Absolutely not, I said. But since motherhood has been exalted to sainthood, I felt that the nonworking mother thought herself better than me.

No, not better, she said. Just different.

Oh, different, I said. I said I hated that word.

We stared at each other for a bit longer and then at the coffee table. She put a hand to her throat and started to rub it. I'm not sure that you know this, Joannie, but you can be very intimidating sometimes.

Intimidating? Me? I thought about all the things I'd been compared to. I told Tami no version of me was that fearsome.

But that's why you're intimidating. Look at all that you've accomplished. You're completely unafraid to plow right on ahead when most of us would be. I want you to have it all, I really do, and thinking ahead for our collective futures, your brother and I also don't want you to be alone. We don't want your mother to be alone. So, with your career now set, is it not time to shift your goals?

I didn't give her a straight answer and she didn't press me. Enough time passed that we both stood up and went back into the kitchen where everyone else was. My mother was sitting by the island with her hot water and phone, a cloud of steam around her. Fang had just come downstairs, hair wet from a shower, and started the coffee. My nephews had found some pool toys in the closet and were whacking one another with foam noodles.

—

ON MARCH 1, A woman traveling back from Iran became New York State's first reported case. A French health official advised against cheek kissing, or *la bise,* and handshakes. The U.S. surgeon general tweeted, Seriously, people—STOP BUYING MASKS! They are NOT effective in preventing the general public from catching #Coronavirus. A Washington State man was the first American to die from it.

When I checked my inbox that week, a deluge of messages

from the board of directors at both West Side Hospital and our sister East Side branch laid out the changes to come. Intensive care units would be expanding, some to entire floors, and in worst-case scenarios to lobbies, atriums, meaning that in worst-case scenarios atrium cafés would have to close.

I wasn't shocked that something like this was happening but that it was, in fact, happening as predicted was somewhat more of a shock. When I told Fang and my mother that I had to return to the city for work, my mother said oh okay, and that was it. She was in a better mood than usual ever since Air China had reached out to her with a spot on an April flight and with the virus in China now handled, her sisters were sending animal videos again, of house pets doing funny, acrobatic things. As our mother chuckled to herself, then went into the living room to scroll through her phone, Fang and I glanced at each other, knowing there was no way that plane was taking off. My brother then asked if I wanted to go back to work, given that I still had two weeks of leave. I said they were officially calling back everyone, even nurse and physician retirees, it was all hands on deck for what would probably be a month-long service, at the very least. Since deaths followed cases by a month, hospital capacity in April would probably hit surge level 1, then level 2, then level very, very bad.

My brother asked if I was worried about getting sick.

I said I'd take all the necessary precautions.

You can stay here as long as you like, he said and I thanked him and he said no need to say thanks.

Thanks, I said and he said no need to say thanks.

I could guess what Fang was going to bring up next since it was already on everyone's mind. America still has a lot of problems, doesn't it, my mother had said the other day, maybe yesterday, while we were channel surfing and a snippet of domestic news came through. Problems that weren't hers to fix but she looked expectantly at me, as if they were mine.

Had I heard what they'd been calling the virus? Fang asked me now and everyone had.

On February 11, the WHO, careful to keep the name scientific, settled on COVID-19, CO for corona, VI for virus, and D for disease, 19 for the year that the disease appeared. Some Americans took the word *corona* to mean something else, and Google searches for the beer virus, or a virus that you could get from simply drinking beer, surged. But some government officials also believed that it was important to keep the American people informed and reminded of where the virus really came from. So, the China virus, the Chinese virus, the kung flu.

Videos had started circulating online, most I couldn't even watch through. Clips of Asian people being attacked in the street and on the subways. Being kicked, pushed, and spat on for wearing masks and being accused of having brought nothing else into the country except disease. The harassed were usually women or the elderly, the easiest target was both. The worst part was that few people around the harassed did anything. No one stopped the crazy white lady from swinging her umbrella at an older woman's covered face or from pointing the umbrella at the woman like a gun. Proud to be an American. Go back to China. Neither Fang nor I mentioned these events to our mother but it seemed she already knew given how often her friends in China asked if she now felt in perpetual danger. Who wanted to go to America anymore was also their sentiment, when the other side of the world was doing much better and had none of this type of unrest? Every country has its problems, doesn't it? was my mother's only reply, and that she was trying her best to return. What of her two children then? they'd asked. Was she worried about them living in that country all on their own? No mother doesn't worry, but my children are grown adults, and have been for a long time. They can take care of themselves.

My brother felt the attacks would continue, so didn't see a point in my going back. Like most of his stances, he wasn't entirely wrong, and to his question of why go back, I sighed, I shrugged, as if I didn't know. But I did know. I was going back because, for better or worse, this was the job.

Could a family's migratory ways lead each member to find their own sense of belonging? Where did my brother belong if not within his wealth and aspirations to reach the land of giants? Where did I belong if not within the confines of a well-defined job? And where did my mother belong, with her own children or to that other life she and my father had created elsewhere after we'd grown? Home could be many things. It could be both a comfort and a pain. It could exile you for a little while but then demand that you return. I was going back not because I expected anyone to care about me or us, not necessarily to be seen as a good person, a kind person, but because the work needed to get done and I already knew I was a good doctor.

———

I'D ALWAYS HEARD THAT on the day my parents got on that plane for America to start anew, six-year-old Fang had cried, screamed, and had to be pulled away from the departure gate where he had wrapped his hands around the no-family-members-beyond-this-point metal bars. Finger by finger, my aunts had to pry him off the bars and carry him away.

That was also what I saw on deathbeds. Son or daughter. The type of child who, after the algorithm had failed and we had explained that it had failed, went on to shake the parent's arm as if to wake them up. Hey, I'm right here, feel my arm on your arm, my hand on your face; feel my total and complete despair, so come back to me and please don't just leave me behind.

I was already forgetting things about my father. I was forgetting how low his voice could be, how he would mumble and flatten his tones. In truth he could have meant another *chuàng,* besides the one about going off to sea. I should have asked him which he intended, but I never got around to that.

The other *chuǎng* is third tone, not fourth. For this *chuǎng,* we put a horse (马) inside a door (门), such that the character itself, 闯, refers to breaking down barriers and charging through. I was reminded of the Trojan horse, the surprise gift horse outside, but also of horsepower, which now belonged to cars. A green Mustang might be irrefutable American muscle, but so was the driver inside. He was pure American muscle with a Chinese heart. Goodbye, doctor-daughter, goodbye, but also see you again.

—

ON THE FIRST DAY I returned to the city and my classic prewar apartment, I bought and installed a deadbolt. Mainly to prevent cross-contamination and unwanted visitors, and what a comforting series of sounds it was, from the locking of my doorknob to the swinging of deadbolt one then two, to the latching of my safety chain. But from inside, almost every night, I could still hear a knock and Mark's voice, asking if everything with me was all right, given what he was seeing on the news. He couldn't quite believe what was happening and didn't know what to believe. Was all of it real? Or a hoax? Or the media? Things were changing so fast, from open to shut down. Broadway had closed—inconceivable—states of emergency declared, bans on other countries, a toilet paper and a hand sanitizer shortage, to mask or not to mask. So how was I doing in there all by my lonesome? And could I please let him know what I made of the craziness out there or at least tell him that I was okay?

I said everything in here, in my own apartment, was fine. I was alone but I felt safe. I had regained control of this, my domain.

By 6:00 a.m. each day, I left for work. On the walk there, I made eye contact with no one, looked ahead and blankly. I kept my jaw clenched and closed my ears to passing dialogue, any shouts directed at me of possible hate. Then once I was in the hospital, I could relax and greet people, because here too I felt safe.

The first time I saw Reese again, he was, as Madeline had warned, Zenned out, thus eerie to sit beside. He no longer made snide comments, jabs; no spontaneous airing of grievances, epiphanies, or throwing stress balls around people's heads. Meditated for ten minutes in the afternoon. Spoke often about his girlfriend. Hey, Reese, I might've said, and he would reply if I knew that his girlfriend, who worked in fashion, was also severely allergic to shellfish. They had an incident two nights ago with some lobster-flavored risotto, and he almost, but didn't, stabbed her with an EpiPen. She was recovered now. I said good to hear. Then he showed me the new picture of them on his desk, which matched the photo of them on his lock screen. A nice distraction, since ten minutes later I was back on my ICU floor and he on his. We led trainings for other doctors, to teach the cardiothoracic surgeons of difficult poetry, for example, how to operate vents during their redeployment. Overflow beds filled the atrium, and its café temporarily closed. The hospital intercom had been set to loop not just in our units but everywhere: Are you suffering from ARDS, sir, madam? Because if so, we can help.

The face shields were the most uncomfortable. When we took them off at the end of the day, there were deep red rings around our foreheads. Madeline would pass me an aloe wipe and we would sit for a minute in the changing room with the cool cotton draped across our faces. Deep breath in, out, the diaphragm is a muscle and breathing rate is one of the few things you can control. When we had to joke about something, we joked that we were sitting in a spa.

By the third week of service, our floors were full, and despite all the PPE, the exposure was simply too high. Reese got it, then Madeline, then me.

Felt like a hot anvil had been placed on my chest.

During the two weeks I was bolted in, on a regimented schedule of water and antivirals, trying to push the anvil off, I had fever dreams. One of an army of robot vacuums moving in parallel from one side of the room to the other, sweeping in unison, then turning in unison and sweeping back, much like a ballet. In those two weeks, I opened my door only once. I thought I'd heard a knock, but by the time I made it to the door from bed, there was no one on the other side of the peephole. I had already lost my sense of smell and taste, why not hearing and sight? I was delirious, and because hearing is the last sense to go, I thought I was also dead. If I was dead and unaware, then maybe here was my father at the door, coming to welcome me over to the other side. Morbid, yet I was unafraid. It was never the disease that I feared. A physical disease I could handle. Cells, pathology, pain—that was tangible stuff, knowable stuff, at least for me. But I was afraid, I supposed, of meeting my father again and having nothing to say. Tell me all about it, Joan, what have I missed? And I would be so overcome by his presence—that he would have more than two minutes to talk to me, that his car would be indefinitely parked—that I would be stumped. But when I opened the door, just a crack, I knew that I was still alive. There, on my welcome mat, were tins of Spam, packets of Chapagetti, a stack of my mail, and a full box of LaCroix tangerine.

The food was from the other tenants, and the doorman continued putting my mail outside my door.

I didn't tell my mother about being sick, but in case of an emergency I had to tell Fang. I waited for him to say his piece. Instead he asked a few questions about how I was feeling, then told me to send him a daily text. About what? I asked. He said he didn't care; just some proof every day that I was lucid and awake. We started off with a standard set: Hi, I'm up. Fever? Yeah. Temp? I told him. As that number started to go down, he sent a thumbs-up emoji. He sent two thumbs-up. He sent a fist bump.

One day, I found myself better and able, masked and gloved,

to go downstairs and get the mail myself. As I was sifting through the pile, one piece stopped me, a trifold brochure in a familiar calming ocean blue.

West Side Hospital. Why choose us? Our dedicated doctors are among the country's best, and we work around the clock. Day and night, we're always ready to provide you with the highest level of medical care. Just ask one of our own.

I had to look twice. I showed the doorman from a distance, both of us peering out from the tops of our masks. Was this . . . ?

Ms. Joanna, that's you.

No, it couldn't be.

Our very own important person, he said, and gave me a quick salute.

The cover showed an Asian woman with one hand gripping the ECMO's cart handle and the other hand held up, as if asking, What's going on here with this wonderful machine and all that it can do? She wasn't facing the camera but a small group who'd gathered around her. I recognized my medical team, the intern, three residents, the fellow, the pharmacist, the head nurse, but I didn't remember this day, because it had been like any other. The line above my head was about my commitment to the white coat and putting it on. Who had taken this casual, typical picture? Who had sent it to the director? My guess was one of the nurses and that once I was back on service, these same nurses would have strung the brochures up, like a garland, along the front of their bay, just to tease me and to welcome me back from my ordeal. Which wasn't so terrible of an ordeal comparatively, I later told them, though I might've permanently lost my sense of taste and smell. And they passed me a packet of hot sauce. A challenge that some of them were doing, the portion that had been sick and recovered. How many packets could you take? Five? Seven? One nurse could take seven and previously had no tolerance for spice. All this to show that we were strong, made stronger, instead of admitting to what we really were, numb.

—

ENGLISH WORDS COULD TELL a story too. *Pandemonium*. *Pandemonic*. *Pandemic*. Or a demon who has come to pan you.

My mother's April flight was canceled. She sounded resigned when she told me that customer service had booked her on the very next available seat for June. They had asked her to be patient. Hundreds of flights had been canceled, tens of thousands of Chinese nationals were trying to get home, especially international students with time-sensitive visas and immigrants working here with entire families back in China, a loved one dying or sick, not from the virus but from other causes, like cancer or heart disease, like stroke. What a virus has never done is scare other deadly illnesses off.

My mother guessed that she wouldn't be flying back in June either. From June it would get pushed to August, to October, and before she knew it, she would turn seventy and, as her friends had warned, be stuck in this country forever. Even if a vaccine did become available and travel resumed, something else would come up to impede her, like extreme climate change, an apocalyptic flood, and not totally impossible, the Third World War.

But if they did ever let her leave, this would be her last trip to the States, she'd decided, she wouldn't be visiting again.

I too suspected the same, that once she left, it was for good. I asked her over the phone how she felt about that. That should she manage to leave now, we might not be able to see her for several years, with more travel restrictions being put into place. There was a long pause and I thought I'd lost her. Mom? Mom? I said and she tsked and told me to calm down. Come up and see me before October then, she said. But not every weekend, please. We've already spent a good amount of time together, so we also don't want to overdo.

Having finally come to terms with our mother not being happy here, Fang was trying to find her a more reliable ticket. I asked him what was happening to these unreliable ones? How were they still being booked and then canceled?

In March, the number of daily cases in China fell below a hundred. On March 10, Xi Jinping visited Wuhan to declare the fight against the virus a success. Wuhan must be victorious, Hubei must be victorious, and all of China must be victorious, he said, while raising a clenched fist. I thought of my father, of course, and the feeling of tumbling face-first down a steep slope of ice. But to continue being victorious, China would close its borders to other nations just as other nations had first done to her. The new policy from its aviation bureau was called Five-One. All domestic airlines were limited to one international flight per week per country, while foreign airlines could fly into the mainland no more than once per week. The list of approved flights was released in batches, and you wouldn't know until some unknown time prior to your flight date if your flight would actually leave. So, to play the odds, people were buying up dozens of tickets at a time and there were simply not enough. The most indefatigable group (hardy international students, the truly desperate to return) bought tickets elsewhere to Japan or Korea, to India, in hopes of catching a transfer, but once they reached their transfer point, new regulations had gone into effect while they were midair, pausing all flights from that country. China-bound passengers would then have to deboard the plane, wait a few hours, and board the same plane back. Fang and I agreed that we couldn't put our mother through that; it was either a direct flight home or nothing.

Home run, for which nicknames include a homer, a goner, a moon shot, the big fly.

———

THE HOSPITAL CONTINUED TO ban family visits, but families wanted to visit, so we began holding phones and iPads up to the sick, ourselves wrapped in polyphenylene ether, gloved, masked, the iPad shielded, wrapped in plastic, the patient covered in a thin white sheet. Sometimes you had to bring the iPad close to catch the patient's voice and then pull the screen farther out since the relatives were louder.

Close: I love you.

Away: And I love you too, but listen, you're going to be fine, and I'll talk to you tomorrow, okay? At this exact time.

There were some horror stories already. Not at our hospital yet, but elsewhere and abroad. A woman in Italy had been unable to leave her apartment. Her husband had tested positive

and died in their house early the next week. The town's protocol stated that no one was allowed to approach the body until
at least two days had passed. So, the widow was stuck at home
with the body. She was seen on her balcony crying for help.

In my own unit, one exchange between a husband and a
wife caught me off guard. I tried to hold the iPad level but was
already having trouble. The city's death count had been climbing, a reminder of the tired-out truth that the demon will always win. But even if it does win, one still has to try. While
there is no fight against death, there are fights to delay it and to
give a person more time. For my father, after a blow to the
head, it was over. He could not speak or move thereafter, so in
that second, he was already gone. But what would he have said
to my mother had he been given the chance?

Write this down, said Earl, the man who was sick, to his
wife. The kids each have a college account with Janus Henderson. He spelled Janus Henderson out for her, enunciating each
letter. To log in to those accounts, they'll first send my phone a
code. You enter that code and then answer the questions. He
gave her the answers to those questions and the passwords to
input right after.

Earl, the wife said, I'm not writing anything down, I refuse.
Come on, talk to me about something else.

You write it down. Or you call this number—he recited the
number digit by digit—they have advisors. You call that number and someone will help you.

The wife stared blankly at the screen but wasn't writing
anything down. As I was setting the iPad up for the call, test-
ing the video and audio, Earl had told me that this was just a
precaution, this was just him preparing for the worst because

he was the pessimist in the family, his wife the optimist. You'll see, he had said.

Earl was now agitated and trying to move his arms from under the thicket of tubes. For the love of God, get over yourself and pick up a pen. I'm trying to tell you something. I just want you to know what to do.

The wife continued to say nothing, but her eyes were shiny, her mouth a flat line.

I said if it was all the same to them, I could write some of this down. I had good recall and legibility.

Someone write something down, Earl said. He didn't care who.

I found a pen, paper. I had the nurse hold the iPad.

More account names and portfolios. The passwords were mostly numbers, and I knew Earl's birthday, his height and weight, his vitals, but these numbers weren't that. They were the birthdays of his wife and kids, followed by their initials and then a bunch of exclamation marks. Earl advised not doing much with one account but selling some in another. The wife nodded and had covered her mouth with her hand. The last account was for their retirement.

We have an advisor there, Earl said. His name is—now don't laugh, I know you're about to laugh. Please don't. I'm tired, I have a tube up my nose. But his name is Earl, an utter coincidence. Don't run off with him after I'm gone.

The wife did laugh. It was a laugh and then a cry. She said she didn't think she could do any of this without him. He said that she could.

—

DURING MY WALK BACK from the hospital that day, I was, surprisingly, less tense. I told Earl that I would be there tomorrow, and he said he would see me tomorrow, though he wasn't a morning person, so if by chance he was asleep or whatnot, he wished to not be disturbed. Lots could happen in the "whatnot" and what would happen to Earl I couldn't predict. That I couldn't predict many things, at times not even my own thoughts, still unsettled me. That I had to stay on guard and protect myself from both the tangible and intangible tired me to my core. But for a moment some of this unease receded, and with no one else around me, I slowed my pace, unclenched my jaw. I shook out my hands, my father's hands, that had been stuffed into my coat pockets and looked around.

The street I was on had a grocery store, a pharmacy, and a convenience store that had remained open after the closure of nonessential business. Along with new guidelines on how to stay safe, there were still posters in its windows for produce, sales, and, on the outside of the convenience store, ads for the state lottery. PLAY NOW! BUY A TICKET AND TRY YOUR LUCK.

Lotteries were unwinnable in real life but never in movies. There's that children's movie about a chocolate factory and the search for five golden tickets, tucked away in chocolate bars. So, if the airlines failed to provide my mother with a ticket, we could always look for one like that. My mother with her golden ticket, waving it around to celebrate that finally she could go home. But in real life, no win is ever unconditional. Once she left, I would be here again without a mother, and while I'd managed before and would again, I was more aware now of the exchange.

I hadn't seen my father die. I had heard and read the report, the death certificate. I had seen, held, the box of ashes. The two Chinese characters of my name were carved into the stone of his tomb, next to my brother's and under my mother's. But it was also possible that he could be anywhere and that he could still surprise me with when he would turn up.

The convenience store I'd just passed was empty except for a dark-haired man behind the counter, face half wrapped in a bandanna, wiping his counters down with a terrycloth. Here was an essential business, as it had always been, and I stopped for a moment in front of the glass.

Doctor-daughter, you're thinking about me again but there's really no need. Both of us are very busy.

Never too busy for you, Dad.

Then how's it going, non-busy daughter? Tell me all about it.

Haven't figured it all out yet.

But you've figured out some.

Some, yes, a very small piece.

So, tell me about that.

During my last year of med school, ten years ago, the Massachusetts Powerball hit a record high. The prize money was something so ridiculous that no sane government would let you keep it without taking at least half in taxes. My father was still alive and in China, but it was during that strange year of no contact between us. The morning before the Powerball was to be drawn, I was standing in line at a convenience store with my breakfast muffin and orange juice, waiting impatiently to check out so I could sprint right back to work. I hadn't been thinking about my father or mother or brother. I hadn't been thinking about the gulfs within families or the migrations we have to make or the cost of love.

In line ahead of me was an Asian father-daughter pair. As their items were being rung up, the young girl asked her father if they could buy a ticket for the Powerball. A glowing neon sign above the cash register suggested it, and it was a historic lottery with just a two-dollar wager. The father resisted at first, but then gave in. The daughter picked six numbers and then a minute later took the ticket from the cashier with both hands. She probably wouldn't win, and I imagined her father knew that. But what could be said of this seemingly frivolous act, a small paper gift that makes the girl happy, which then makes her father happy, which then spurs a, perhaps, normally stoic dad to express how much he cares about the daughter in ways that she can't yet comprehend. After I'd slid my credit card over to pay for my stuff, I overheard the girl ask what if they did win, what would they buy? They were heading toward the exit and I glanced over at them, the daughter still a head shorter than the father, more engrossed with her ticket of unrealistic promise than with her father's reply. Win? he said. He opened the door for both of them, standing aside to let her go first. But I've already won, I've made a life here.

# ACKNOWLEDGMENTS

THE WRITING OF THIS book would not have been possible without enormous support along the way.

To both Sigrid and Xuefei for your unparalleled goodness. I really don't know how else to thank you except to keep writing.

Linda, for her love and care, the decades of sisterhood, and for letting me tag along on quests for great food. Yuying, Xiaoli, and Briana for patiently answering my many, many questions about medicine, hospitals, and doctors and for their one question back, that this story wasn't going to be about them, was it? Caroline and Jamie for their insights and willingness to read the earliest of bad drafts, sent not even in a Word doc but in snippets of text. Thank you, Hooman and Eric, for showing me what attendings do and letting me come on rounds. Michel, for providing that rare combo of whiskey and legal advice.

To all the great friends made in school, at work, on the Great Hill of Central Park, through science, and through writing, thank you for the happy times, game nights, long walks, meals, letters, and messages that cheered me on. Also, to the students, neighbors, door people who have become friends, and are now, constantly, asking me about my next book, thanks for keeping me on schedule.

I have a great agent in Joy Harris, and could not have found a better advocate, sounding board, anchor. Many thanks to everyone in that agency, especially Adam Reed.

I have a great editor in Robin Desser. Thanks for the phone calls, the discussions, and, of course, the notes that made this book infinitely better than I could have. To Clio Seraphim for her astute eye, calming demeanor, and exceptional tech skills. But what I will miss most about our editorial process is sending both of you funny gifs. The entire Random House team, I'm floored by the warmth that you have shown this book and me.

To Michael, my heart. Thanks for reading every scene about seven and a half times and for listening to the long list of my concerns, many repetitive, and for reminding me that it will all be okay. Mr. Biscuit, thanks for being handsome and growing the world's longest eyelashes. Finally, I'm indebted to my earliest family for the gift of a second language and home in Chinese. To my grandmother and late grandfather, I love and miss you. To my parents for being there from the very start and for showing me how to persevere with grit, to humor with wit.

# JOAN IS OKAY

## WEIKE WANG

A BOOK CLUB GUIDE

# A NOTE FROM THE AUTHOR

Dear Reader:

I created Joan to explore, and to help me understand, the encroaching pressures on a person like her. She is an amalgam of my own ambitions and frustrations. She is a mirror of many of my peers. I did not start writing creatively until college, and the first characters that I created on the page were nameless, raceless, and sexless because I believed that I would be doing them a great disservice by giving them identities. With identity comes identity problems. Their enforced invisibility was undoubtedly an extension of my own.

The concepts that permeate my work are there because I live with them every day. There were long periods of my schooling when I could not escape hearing the word "sacrifice" and how much had been sacrificed for me to have the opportunities that I did. In return, I could not forsake those who had made that possible for me. I could not deviate from the plan.

What was the plan? The skill-based world of science used

to be much more familiar to me than the world of writing. I was trained in STEM and for many years prepared myself for a career in medicine. I wavered in this regard, but Joan does not. In some ways, she is the person that I'd hoped to be—an ideal worker who thrives on work, embodies it completely, and never wishes to be disturbed.

Joan sits at the intersection of many experiences that I personally have found painfully confusing and angering. There is the Asian American experience, the immigrant experience, the woman-in-science experience, the mental health experience. Groups who are different are often labeled as such and feel the heavy expectation to fit in. Fitting in is as it sounds: you must trim yourself down to fit a mold. Yet Joan has willingly done that to herself and integrated herself into the hospital because she admires the supposed meritocracy of it all. She believes that through this straight and steadfast path she can circumvent her other identities of being an Asian American woman, a child of struggling immigrants, a person with familial obligations and cultural roots. This is not true and cannot be true. Said another way, I created Joan to test her. There are obstacles already in her life that she has trained herself to ignore.

The novel's concept and first drafts took place before the onset of the global pandemic. Afterward, I found myself writing about a Chinese American ICU doctor in the light of a virus that has inflicted widespread disease and fear. I watched from the sidelines as my friends, these lauded model minorities and assimilation success stories, reported to their hospital posts where they were questioned by patients and peers for their patriotism. In response, I felt an urgency to reflect on the contemporary upheaval and ugliness, which are not so much new as they are simply brushed aside by their sufferers out of a conditioned desire to not cause trouble. As a character, Joan is equal parts Asian American success and failure. She strives to never cause trouble until she does, and once trouble arrives, she must finally reckon with who she is.

A most heartfelt thanks for choosing *Joan Is Okay* for your book club. I'm thrilled, honored, and hope you enjoy the experience of getting to know her through your discussion.

—Weike Wang

# QUESTIONS AND TOPICS
# FOR DISCUSSION

1. Joan is a successful ICU doctor, a first-generation Chinese American, a daughter and sister, a workaholic, and a happily single woman in her thirties. How are these different parts of her identity in harmony with one another? How are they dissonant?

2. *Joan Is Okay* takes place in 2019, in the months leading up to the Covid-19 pandemic. How does this timing influence the events of this novel? How would the book be different if set well before, during, or after Covid-19?

3. As Joan recalls memories from her childhood and her relationship with her parents, she notes "Berating is love, and here I was at thirty-six, still being loved." Discuss the family dynamics at the core of this novel. How do Joan, Fang, and their mother show each other love? What do they withhold or hide from one another? How does this dynamic change after Joan's father dies, and by the time they are all in Greenwich together?

**4.** Joan thinks a lot about being Chinese American outside of China. At one point she says she doesn't consider herself too Chinese, and rarely goes to China to visit. In another instance, Joan reflexively apologizes to a nurse for speaking Chinese. Yet she also doesn't feel that the phrase "Proud to be an American" really applies to her. Discuss how Joan grapples with her Chinese heritage and identity. What is important for readers to see within her internalized struggle?

**5.** *Joan Is Okay* is filled with sharp, satirical humor. What scenes or moments made you laugh? What does humor add to the overall effect of the story?

**6.** Joan is a woman in a male-dominated workplace. How does that manifest through her relationship with Reese? How does she navigate this? How is she treated differently from her male peers? What did you think of the portrayal of Human Resources and corporate wellness initiatives?

**7.** "History repeats itself," Wang writes. "Asians are often pitted against other Asians, and even citizenship can't always save you." How did this novel make you reflect on the treatment of Asian Americans in the United States, particularly in the wake of the coronavirus? How does this tie into Joan's memory of the father and daughter buying the lottery ticket at the end of the novel?

**8.** Wang writes, "The price of success is steep and I've never been able to distinguish it from the feeling of sacrifice." Why do you think Joan equates success and sacrifice? Do you feel similarly? Why or why not? What does success look like for the different characters in this novel?

**9.** *Joan Is Okay* depicts two different perspectives on the immigrant experience: Joan's and her brother's. Discuss how Joan and Fang each feel about being immigrants. Why do you think they react differently? How do they feel about each other's paths? How does being an immigrant impact their life choices?

10. At the end of the book, Wang writes, "Home could be many things. It could be both a comfort and a pain. It could exile you for a little while but then demand that you return." Where does home truly lie for Joan? What does home mean to you?

11. Though Joan's father is a passive character in the book, he is still very much a significant player. Discuss the influence Joan's father has on her character. To what extent is Joan changed (or not changed) by the grief she feels after her father dies?

12. How does *Joan Is Okay* compare to the "classic" immigrant novel? Explain the role class plays in the story. What themes and expectations does this novel affirm and/or upset?

13. Discuss the characters: Joan, our protagonist, is very unique and striking, but so are many of the secondary and tertiary figures. How is Joan's relationship to her father different from her relationship with her mother? How do Joan and her brother, Fang, compare?

14. What did you think about Joan's relationship with her neighbors, particularly Mark? At first, he seems to be a foil for Joan, but he's also one of the many forces in her life insisting her lifestyle is unsatisfactory. Why does Joan let him force his way into her life? What does it mean to have your sensibilities questioned in your own home?

15. Reading is often about finding empathy for others. Discuss the empathy you had (or didn't have) for the characters in *Joan Is Okay*. What did you take away from reading this novel?

Weike Wang was born in Nanjing, China, and grew up in Australia, Canada, and the United States. She is a graduate of Harvard University, where she earned her undergraduate degree in chemistry and her doctorate in public health. Her first novel, *Chemistry,* received the PEN/Hemingway Award for Debut Fiction, the *Ploughshares* John C. Zacharis First Book Award, and a Whiting Award. She is a "5 Under 35" honoree of the National Book Foundation and her work has appeared in *The New Yorker*. She currently lives in New York City.

weikewangwrites.com
Instagram: @weikewang

Read more by

# Weike Wang

Winner of the PEN/Hemingway Award and a Whiting Award

---

## One of the Best Books of the Year:
NPR, *Entertainment Weekly*, Ann Patchett on *PBS NewsHour*,
Minnesota Public Radio, *PopSugar*, Maris Kreizman,
*The Morning News*

**"Winningly original . . .** pithy, casually brilliant . . .
fresh and intimate and mordantly funny."
—*Entertainment Weekly*

---

**Available wherever books are sold**   VintageBooks.com